Julian Hawthorne

Love is a Spirit

A Novel

Julian Hawthorne

Love is a Spirit
A Novel

ISBN/EAN: 9783337001674

Printed in Europe, USA, Canada, Australia, Japan

Cover: Foto ©Andreas Hilbeck / pixelio.de

More available books at **www.hansebooks.com**

LOVE IS A SPIRIT

A Novel

BY

JULIAN HAWTHORNE

NEW YORK
HARPER & BROTHERS PUBLISHERS
1896

LOVE IS A SPIRIT

I

" Thy Hornbook I cannot spell—
In me all Wisdom's Secrets dwell.
Prove me Fool by Rule of Thumb—
Blind without me were Heaven, and dumb."

FOR an hour before he came the girl had been sitting nearly motionless on the bench overlooking the rose-garden.

She leaned against a pillar; her right arm, bare to the elbow, lay along the broad marble balustrade of the veranda; the coolness of the smooth stone was grateful in the tropic afternoon. It was an afternoon that drowsed and dreamed and distilled fragrance. The May rains had been sending herald showers before them for a week past, and

sky, mountains, trees, the whole flowery voluptuous earth, were lulled in sensuous delight. Beauty was everywhere.

Beauty was everywhere; but though the
full white lids of the girl's eyes were only
half closed, she was unregardful of things
without. She was gazing quietly into the
realms of her soul.

The spiritual world, inhabited unawares by
the human spirit even during life in the body,
is at rare intervals open to consciousness.
Ordinarily, as the ripple on the surface of
water obscures the secrets of the depths, so
physical sense obscures our vision of the inward life; but the depths are there, and the
recesses of the soul — let what turmoil may
prevail without—remain forever tranquil.

For conflict belongs to transitory existence
only; the immortal is unassailable, and moves
unceasingly forward in a current too profound to be perceived. Beings whom no end
threatens, who after eternities of divine activ-
ity to beatify their fellows and beautify their

world find themselves immeasurably more able than at first — for such there are no clashings of will with law, no discrepancy between means and ends, no discords. They hear the rhymings of truth with love, see forms of use transfigured into beauty, and their hearts beat in the rhythm of common effort towards universal good.

Upon this inner world, through the portals of her virgin heart, the girl looked. Her heart, though virgin, was not vacant. Pure youth is always weaving, out of its beliefs, intuitions, and aspirations, the image of an ideal being. To each of us the opposite sex is a mirror reflecting the reverse image of our own best selves, which, because reversed, is made pregnant of the life which isolation never can engender. Over this image of all lovableness the maiden throws the glamour of whatever is nobly masculine, while the man consecrates it with womanliness.

But the image requires a concrete nucleus on which to model it. Some fair face or tender voice, some manly look or picturesque action, gives the hint; and straightway the creation glows with life and beauty.

Fully to realize the ideal is a more critical matter. Yet, as a child arrays with the graces of its imagination the first block of wood that comes to hand, and finds it lovable, so has the rankest pretender a fair chance of being accepted as the true prince or princess. But while the child may throw aside its doll, the fable of Frankenstein pictures the plight of the deceived lover.

But how happens it that, in a question to answer which the finest faculties of the soul are addressed, mistake should be so often made? The rankest obtuse on‑looker may see at a glance the error to which the exqui‑ site organization of the lover is incorrigibly blind.

Omne ignotum pro magnifico. Youth and maiden, in the mystic glory of pubescence, are not as men and women of the world, cate‑ chising the very Eros and Psyche; rather are they prone to canonize the devil. The more they abhor evil in the abstract, the less ready are they to credit it in the concrete.

Moreover, as the full cloud yearns to give itself in rain, as the winged bird fain would fly, as the trained athlete chafes to put forth his strength, so must needs the potent lover approve potency by act. This limitless wealth was given to spend, and spent it shall be, though cast at the feet of swine. The first impulse of love is to give; the craving to receive a like gift in return comes not till afterwards.

It is in that craving that the frailty of the complex emotion lies. To love is safety and increase, for its prototype is the Creator; but to suffer love is perilous, since its dependence is upon the creature. Yet to this end were we born—to love and be beloved; the passion is as sweet as the action; and both must mingle to make the full draught of human happiness. But what marvel if, seeking for our birthright, rich in instinct and poor in experience, we are misled by wandering fires?—or can any danger, incurred for such a birthright, be too great?

The girl suddenly changed her position, and looked towards the right. The height on which the house stood sloped abruptly to a plain, bordered by a forest, from which emerged a road that crossed the plain in the direction of the house. A man on horseback had ridden forth from the wood and was cantering down the road.

She watched his approach with an intentness that made her soul shine through her eyes. There was a tightness about her heart, caused by wide emotions surging through it, as ocean tides rush through a Hellespont. With a sigh the pressure was relieved, and sparkling currents of delight frolicked through her veins, and changed the quick pallor of her cheeks to rose. Her brain was confused with vague images of joy at hand. She was unconscious of her body; she never

knew that she strained her soft hands together till the serpent's head on her ring bit
the flesh. Physical sensation was dominated
by the music in her soul, made by love, which
is a spirit.

II

" 'Shall Impotence the Burden bear,
  While Strength goes free as weightless air?'
Aye, since all Powers, mete and bound
In yonder helpless Babe are found!''

BUT though lovers are wont to lament the intractability of matter, it is yet a dispensation for which—did their wisdom equal their ardor—they should be passing grateful.

We do not give infants naked poniards to play with. Sharp points and edges must be sheathed to them until they learn prudence. Now, the scimitar of Saladin itself is dull beside the disincarnate soul; and mortal life is the sheath divinely appointed to afford us opportunity to learn the handling thereof, without too much risk of cutting our fingers or stabbing ourselves to the heart.

Lovers cry out against the weariness and delay of time and space, which separate them by hours and days, by seas and mountains ; and denounce the clumsiness of the flesh, which is always deflecting or misinterpreting the lightning messages of the mind. But these obstacles are in truth beneficent counsellors, which not only guard the priceless privilege of second thought, but offer us the jewels of patience, fortitude, reason, faith, and hope — jewels created by our struggle against the inertia of circumstance and the subtleties of temptation.

Even though, as the old theologians maintained, there be damnation in matter, it is certain that salvation would be impossible without it. Conceive yourself, if you can, born inexperienced into a state of being where thought is presence ; where the interiors of heart and mind are pictured in the exterior environment ; where there is no interval between desire and accomplishment, will and act ; above all, where that balance between good and evil which we call free will, which is the very sculptor of character, is non-existent—imagine yourself launched in such an ocean, with every sail of hereditary evil spread, with no pilot memory to stand at the helm, and no warning chart of the deadly whirlpool of selfhood to admonish your course withal. Where and how would that voyage end?

No; to be an angel, even in the proper world of angels, is no easy thing. Mortal existence, whether merry or not, can hardly be too long or too material to fit us for such an undertaking. Even the seeming empty forms and ceremonies of social intercourse are precious leading-strings and danger-signals, without which fatal calamities would be yet more frequent than they are. Blessed, then, be the body, and all that it involves! in itself it is an unadulterated benefit to its owner, and whatever mischief he contrives to accomplish through it would have been indefinitely more virulent but for its restraint.

III

"Costliest raiment purse can buy
Flatters not like lover's eye,
Which pranks its object in such trim
As beggars Earth, makes Heaven dim."

MEANWHILE the horseman has passed the gate, reached the door, dismounted, and traversed the central hall of the house. He stepped out on the veranda; as he did so the girl rose from the bench with the air of having been unexpectedly aroused from reverie.

In a world of pure spirit the interposition of such a shield would have been impracticable. But, in fact, this actual moment of meeting hands and eyes affected her as an anticlimax. No real man could ever hope to rival his own heroic figure in the heart of the woman who loves him and has just been thinking how divine he is! Nor can any encounter of mortal lovers fulfil their forecast of it. But it must, moreover, be noted that in this case love had not overtly been in question on either side. The man was an agreeable acquaintance of comparatively recent introduction — a welcome help towards disposing of the diminishing remnant of the tropic season; and the woman was a charming girl, fresh and unsophisticated, in whom a gentleman who had had some experience of the hollowness of the world could not but feel a genial interest.

Such at least was the appearance, in this world of appearances, to be invalidated by conjecture only. It is wonderful under how many veils and disguises this spirit, love, conceals itself, as though aware of its own dangerous quality, and solicitous to protect its votaries to the last. Albeit the unrivalled and unique despot of mankind, it may plausibly be construed as indifference, coquetry, compassion, friendship, courtesy, rudeness, contempt, and hatred ; nor are any so long blind to its true character as are those particular persons to whom its recognition is of most vital consequence.

" Here I am again, you see, Miss Yolande, ready to risk wearing out my welcome! Have I done it, at last ?"

With what a lovely frankness she put forth from the shoulder her virginal arm, letting it fall again to her side, after her hand had touched his! What maidenly dignity she had ; and how formidably searching was the slow, shy regard of her long, dark eyes!

" You will sooner wear out your horse's shoes than your welcome here, Mr. Strathspey !"

How this man made other things seem far off or invisible! He was real—almost too real! It was hard to think beyond the outlines of his figure — that light, athletic figure, booted and spurred, with head erect, and lean, masculine features. Something in him

—whether or not you quite liked it — held you.

"I'll have him shod with chilled steel henceforth."

"Why not ride Pegasus, who needs no shoes at all, and goes swift as thought?"

"By Jove! if I only could catch him! But I am a man who is obliged to keep on the earth; the winged horse would throw me at the first bound, and rid you of me once for all."

How keen and yet soft was his way of looking at one! How handsome he was when he smiled! It showed the strength and fineness of his face. What a thorough man he was, from head to heel!

"Come on a tortoise, if you must—only come."

Never was there another face so singular and absorbing as hers. The subtlety of its forms defied definition. A touch of the Greek, but with a soul in it; a far suggestion of the Sphinx, but spiritualized. Or was it pure modern, the flower of eighteen centuries of Christendom? Ah, well, it was Yolande—expression incarnate : a shimmering flow of mysteries and meanings—of mysteries that were meanings, and of meanings that were mysteries.

" Will you have some tea?"

" No, thanks. Our talk sha'n't be strangled with beverages."

Their talk! What had they been saying to each other? Words are wheels, on which you roll along and dream other things. But that deep voice of his vibrated in her ears, and reached a secret place low in her bosom, whence she took her breath. It said things interior to words, which she loved to hear.

" Shall we walk in the rose-garden, then? and you can smoke a cigar."

" By Jove, yes!—the rose-garden. I never yet had roses enough."

" Come with me and you shall have them."

IV

"Dawn's delicate Disdain, rank Noon,
  Eve's Roses, star-discovering Night,
Sea, holy Hills—but hold my tune,
  Quick creatures of my Will and Sight."

S they entered the garden the sun
sank behind the battlements of a
thunder-cloud, which the powers of the air
had been building along the western horizon.

The garden might have covered a couple
of acres; but the rose-bushes were so high
and thick, and the paths such Dædalian
windings, that, once in the garden, you lost
all sense of its extent. Its dimensions and
beauty became subjective of the measure
and quality of the beholder's soul, and to
these two, at this time, may have appeared
to touch the verge of the infinite. The roses

of all Persian poetry were here, and the conditions (so thought the visitor) such as the
imagination of a Saadi could not have sur-
passed.

Tropical twilights are brief, and the phan-
tasmagory of the sunset marshalled itself
swiftly. Early in the afternoon there had
been a storm amidst the western mountain-
tops, too distant for its thunderous accom-
paniment to reach the ear, though the lightning flashes had been visible, and—swept by
wind-gusts in aerial curves—the brown, filmy
curtains of descending rain. All the while,
high above the shadowy tumult, the upper
sky was serene and pure, with shreds of
snowy cloud, diaphanous as frost on a win-
dow-pane, drawn out upon its tender blue.

At the going down of the sun the storm,
broken into fragments, drifted in heavy
masses athwart the clear luminousness beyond, and gathered in frowning walls and
towers of vaporous masonry. These in their
turn were shattered, and the detached heaps

2

of ruin assumed the likeness of amorphous monsters and grotesque figures, the rout of a titanic battle. By imperceptible degrees disintegrating and recombining, they were tossed in darkling relief against the horizon.

The translucency of the lower atmosphere was tinged with hues faint and delicate at first as the rainbow shadings on a fairy's wings, but ever glowing and kindling, till you would have thought that the jewelled walls of the Celestial City had dissolved in air, and were flowing in prismatic tides above the earth. A broad river of spiritual chryso-prase stretched along the west, islanded with gold and crimson, and with shores of fretted violet, upon which the sinister le-gions of the storm pursued one another with wild contortions. Towards the zenith the sky still kept its azure; and the moon, three days old, both her delicate horns point-ing upwards, seemed slowly to approach the earth.

The girl and the man sauntered side by

side along the winding paths. The bushes, bourgeoning outward, inclined the two fig- ures towards each other in gentle recurrent contacts. Beauty, and the hour, wrought an interior mood, from which, after a while, they reached an imaginative vein, half playful, half serious.

" It is like hearing distant music when you are in a reverie, to see that," said she, indi- cating by a movement of the head the glo- ries of the sky.

" It makes me think of a battle in Homer," he returned—" the heroes struggling together gigantically ; and those shadowy figures hov- ering above them are the Immortals, encour- aging the Trojans or the Greeks."

" The plains of Troy never looked so beautiful as those spaces of green and rose. Such shapes and colors are like a picture of thoughts that never can be spoken."

" It is ominous—that dark wrack," said he, "It is like the shadow of mortality, that looms and passes."

"You cannot separate it from the glory
behind it," she answered. "We ourselves
are darkness; but the light that is not we
gives us meaning and nobility."

That soft touch of her shoulder against
his arm—it was more than a touch; it lin-
gered, and made every nerve a duct of sweet-
ness, pouring like honey into his heart. Was
she aware of it? Was not the very sweet-
ness due to the harmony between them?
Were they not thinking each other's thoughts
—alive with the same emotions? If not, all
intuition was a lie.

But no! there could be and must be nothing of the sort. It was well for him to love
her—she could represent for him all pure and
lovely things; but it would be far from well
were she to love him. Let this vindicate
the worthiness of his devotion — that by no
word or intimation would he ever permit her
to suspect it. She did not love him; she felt
in him merely the generous confidence of a
girl in an honest man much older than her-

self. She loved beauty, romance, noble conduct, and high ideals; she had never sought
or found an individual embodiment of these
qualities. She recognized and enjoyed in
him an apt and friendly sympathizer with
the graceful abstractions in which her mind
loved to dwell—and that was all. There
could be, for her, no peril in their intercourse; and as for him, if he chose to expose
his heart to the delicious stab of her unconscious dagger, that was his affair.

Moreover, if this were self-abnegation, still
more was it wisdom. Sunlight on a distant
mountain-summit is more exquisite than that
which falls around us; and so is love that cannot be ours than that which is in our embrace.
The severest test of the soul's strength is
possession. True passion is a paradox—fire
burning in ice; within that medium it is opaline and divine; but once the ice is melted
nothing but an earthly flame remains.

So they sauntered on, and were hidden
out of sight amongst the roses.

V

"Beauty cheapening Arts,
      Fragrance Joy bestows;
  Love in virgin Hearts
      Seeking—I found a Rose!"

THE heavy blooms, weighting the slender sprays, bent them across the path; the thorns caught the thin fabric of her white dress, and he pricked his fingers in freeing her from them. They smiled at the thorns, but the flowers recalled them to a serious felicity. Roses hung higher than their heads; roses swept their hands as they passed; they trod upon fallen showers of rose petals. There were roses of many colors — crimson, pink, white, yellow, in countless delicate gradations; small and fairy-like, sumptuous and large; some shut up tight in baby buds, others half unfolding their glowing fingers from their golden hearts, others again disclosing the treasure with a lovely frankness, as who should say, "We are the flowers of love— love us!" But these were fragile; at a touch they made themselves into a rosy shower, and were not. The buds were a promise unconsummated; only rarely bloomed a perfect rose, vigorous and flawless, which could be plucked and smelled, and yet endure.

She gave him such a one, remarking, "It will last till you get home; and a rose that lasts an hour will live forever, for in an hour we can learn to know it well enough to recognize it in heaven."

As she turned to him with the last words his heart beat stronger; so close to his was the gleaming beauty of her eyes, the warm fragrance of her mouth. Every feature of her presence wrought upon him: the flowing curves about her waist and bosom, the undulation of her supple flank, the pale glow of her arms and bust through the semi-trans-

parent lawn, the rhythm of her breathing.
How well she set her foot upon the ground,
the elastic knee straightening as she swayed
forward to the next step! Oh, innocent al-
lurement and sweet health of virginal womanhood! Oh, mystic sex, the power of powers!

"There would be no roses," said he, "if
it were not for girls like you."

She smiled her recognition of that spiritual appreciation. When she smiled no man
could help but worship her. The light of
her happiness seemed to radiate through
her face. How could anything mortal be
so heavenly bright?

Happy, in truth, she was. The man beside her stimulated her soul like an elixir.
She felt a personal delight in all appertaining to him : the manly carriage of his shoulders; the firm, shaven cheeks and chin; his
hands, strong and full of meaning, with fine,
crisp hair on the wrists and the back. How
beautiful to be so strong and fearless—to be a

man! Were there in her, or in the world, any good that he had not, how joyfully would she bestow it on him! He could crush her in a moment, if he would; but he would not— he would protect her, because he was good and she was helpless. How beautiful to be protected by him, to surrender to him, to let his nobility and generosity decree her laws and acts! Till now she had valued her independence above all things; what delight, then, to give it up to him! But perhaps he would not care for her gifts. Truly, he did not need them; he was sufficient to himself. Ah, but there were sweet things that she could do for him which he could not but be glad to accept, let him be as proud as he might.

These thoughts and feelings were not outwardly manifested, nor were they even in the foreground of her mind; training and heredity kept them back. But they were more real than what was suffered to appear. And, after all, they were manifest, though not by

conventional signs. Essential woman is or-
ganized emotion; in the presence of what
she loves how can she be hidden? And
what had Yolande to fear? If he loved her,
all was well; if he did not, nothing in this
world could make her feel a wound, no
other good could make life tolerable. It
were an insult to love to imagine such a
thing. But the dignity of womanhood was
in her keeping? Could dignity be based on
such a tenure? The highest glory of woman was to love; if she loved in vain, it was
death, perhaps, but how was it disgrace?
It would be disgrace to fear such a death.
It would be sweet to die.

As the dusk fell the perfume of the garden became more sensibly delicious, as if the
visibility of the roses had been transmuted
into fragrance. It was a delicate swoon of
odors, in which what was material seemed
to pass into the plane of spirit. The two
entered a path which led them along the
boundary of the enclosure; over the wall

extended the boughs of orange-trees, laden with blossoms. He plucked a twig of these; and then they left the garden, remounted the veranda, and sat down together beside the marble balustrade.

" The last of the sunset and the first of the moon," said the girl; " I like this hour best."

" Have you often sunsets like that here in the tropics—and such moons ?"

" They are best now, just before the rains. The air seems to me like a mighty nation preparing for a crusade. There are signs and portents, and gatherings of the hosts, and splendid councils of the princes in their shining armor, and processions with streaming banners and rainbow robes; and once in a while dark hours of humiliation and prayer; and then dazzling tumults of hope and rejoicing. I am always forgetting that you are from the North," she added ; " but, after all, all I know of you is that you are Mr. Strathspey. Were you never in our island till now ?"

"I should like to forget that I was ever anywhere else," replied he, after a pause.

"Have you been unhappy?" she asked, her low voice falling lower with innocent sympathy.

He turned his head and looked at her with a certain pregnant vehemence in his eyes. But he restrained himself; this was perilous ground. To love was to hold sacred. Unless this girl was sacred to him, heaven—which meant immortality with her hereafter—was closed to him forever. And he must not only himself abstain from speaking or acting what looked towards love, but must divert her also from the path in which (as he could no longer but be aware) she was beginning to walk.

"My child," said he, suddenly assuming the smile of a man of the world, "I don't set up to anything unique or wonderful; and let me tell you that nothing could be more wonderful and unique than a man, old enough to be your father, who had never been unhap-

py." To himself he added, "Come! that was
well put."

But she was at once conscious of the descent
to artificiality. "Why do you treat me so?"
she demanded, with the terrible sincerity possible only to the pure and single - minded.
She looked at him seriously and unswervingly. "Even a child may help a man, if he will
let her—and I am more than a child!"

He dropped his eyes, and said, uneasily,
"The worst of a fellow's past is that it becomes the rudder of his future — the pilot
that steers him, rather. If I told you—"
He broke off. A dozen words more would
have swept danger from their path forever;
but he could not get them out; they seemed
too brutal. They would be irrevocable, too;
and the danger, identical with her ignorance
of the truth, was to him the one sweet left in
the world, and he lacked resolution to destroy it.

"If I told you all the annoyances life has
brought me, it would not only bore you, but

I should get the blues myself. I think it more sensible to enjoy the present. Don't you?"

"We must understand a thing to enjoy it," was her reply, "and you said just now that the present is made of the past. But it wasn't your biography I asked to know, but the deeper thing—the spiritual part. As it would be if we met in heaven," she added, after musing for a moment.

"You must come down to earth if we are to meet," said he; "I'm afraid I can't go up to you."

"Oh, I am here," she returned, turning to him with a lovely smile and gesture, as if to say, "Touch me, and see."

The next moment she blushed. He passed a hand over his face, and said, "Even here there are obstacles. I am overstaying my time." He took out his watch with an apology, and glanced at it. "By Jove! I must go."

He half rose. "No!" she exclaimed, vehemently; and involuntarily obeying the throb of her heart, her hands went forth with a gesture, as if to keep him in his seat.

"Don't leave me alone," she went on, quickly. "The others will be back before long. Why — and you didn't smoke your cigar, after all! You must have it now: let me get you a match."

He put his hand on her wrist. "Stay where you are," said he.

The change in his voice affected her as much as his touch; he perceived the vibration in her nerves, and, slowly relinquishing his grasp, affected to search his pockets for a cigar.

"It's all going wrong again, but I can't help it," he said to himself. "Perhaps a smoke may straighten me out. You're sure you won't mind?" he added aloud, pausing with the poised match.

She only shook her head, gazing intently at him through the dusk. Her bosom rose and fell at last with a heave no longer to be repressed. She was a-tremble to the marrow, but happier, she thought, than she had ever yet been. She felt as if she were being carried through the air whirlingly, but to a place of peace and delight. As he lit the match and held the flame before his eyes, she swiftly lifted her clasped hands to her face and pressed against her cheek the wrist which he had touched. When the veil of flame had passed she appeared quite serene and composed in the young moonlight.

He cleared his throat, and inhaled and slowly emitted a cloud of smoke.

"It's an awfully lovely evening, sure enough," he observed.

"Yes. See that strange cloud against the bar of orange sky in the west. It looks like a head—a man's head."

"Do you think so? Strikes me more like—" He checked himself suddenly.

"Were you going to say, like a woman's? Yes—perhaps it does—now. But I often

wonder I never see a cloud face that I recognize. Does this look like some one you
know?"

But he was silent, staring at the face as a
man stares at his enemy. In a few moments,
of course, it dissolved, and became but a
formless cloud drifting across the fading
western glow.

"I beg your pardon!" he said, turning to
her. "Yes—queer things, likenesses. No—
I can't say it did."

It was the shadow of the secret he would
not tell.

VI

" They win that yield ; who love, withdraw ;
    Veiled Reverence Things hid shall see.
    I slew the Slave who feasted me,
To share thy Princely Pulse and Straw."

THEY leaned against the marble railing fronting each other, but looking out upon the rich obscurity of the garden. The moon had begun to reign.

Though so young, her tropic vitality made her mightier than in the north. The crescent of light hung below, a curving chalice accurately poised. Its marvellous brightness made it seem of larger radius than the dark remnant of the sphere which was upheld within it, an orbed jewel of sullen violet. The brightness, though so effulgent, was not cold and whitely virginal, like the icy gleam of Diana's eyes when the gaze of doomed

Actæon burned in breathless ecstasy upon what had been veiled even from Immortals. No ; this was the Diana of Endymion, warm with celestial passion, forsaking the austere barrenness of chastity and glowing divinely radiant from the first draught of her lover's manhood. The light of her glory mingled with the earth rather than shone upon it, and everywhere wrought delicious mystery. It seemed to dissolve the solid planet and to recreate it in forms of spiritual poetry. All was shadowy and plastic ; the great mountains undulated a vaporous film ; the plain was an expanse of luminous dusk, through which one might plunge into a magic underworld ; the darker masses of the trees appeared to rest like clouds upon the bosom of this terrestrial firmament, and to be alike unsubstantial. Nor was this, as in our thinner climate, a vision of mere black and white ; there was the eloquence of color, voluptuous and of infinite subtlety, like memory of music in a dream.

"Oh, I love it!" cried Yolande — for whom, unlike her distraught companion, no barriers imprisoned her soul from present delight in nature's innocent, profound apocalypse. "I could not understand the earth, or believe in it, but for such times as these, when it seems as if a breath might blow it away, and leave nothing but heaven!"

"You seem very sure of there being a heaven," said he. "Do you know that some people think there is none?"

"No heaven? There can be nothing else —except that very thought that there is none."

He brushed off the ash of his cigar on the marble.

"I need to feel the solid reality of the planet," he said.

"There can be but one reality," she answered, "and this"—she sent her hands abroad with a sweeping gesture, and brought them back till the palms met—"this cannot be it. Think how terrible if it were, in spite of its beauty—no, because of it."

"Yes, of course. . . . Nature the illusion of sense . . ." mumbled he, perplexed to find himself fingering the half-forgotten metaphysics of distant college days. He could not get in touch with the spontaneous vision of this intuitive soul. Yolande was not a metaphysician, she was a spirit.

"I love sunshine," she went on, "but I shall love it with my whole heart only in heaven. Here moonlight is best; it is the truer light for earth. The sun makes all so clear you can hardly remember it is but an image, after all; but the moon gives you back the unreality that is the truth."

"After asking me to stay with you, you soar away from me," he said, after a little. "My dwelling has been in what you call the Unreality—I could find a harder name for it —and I have no wings; so these angelic flights of yours make me lonely."

She turned slowly, inclining her body towards him. Yes, there was a heaven indeed, and that supple figure and moonlit face and low voice were of its sound and substance.

" Lonely ?" she repeated, slowly.

At this moment a truth presented itself to Strathspey's mind.

Time and space as discipline are guides to heaven, but misused become prompt and plausible ministers of the devil. Though the inertia of the body may as well hinder as help good impulses, and thus negatively protect the soul, yet this otherwise friendly associate of ours owns a fatal power accorded to no other agent in any plane of existence — the power, namely, to effect desecrations. Between evil and holy in the other world is fixed a gulf impassable; but here an embodied hell may embrace an incarnate heaven, or thrust its foul presence into the penetrail of the Lord's temple. For these crimes the penalty is eternal.

Strathspey need but put forth a hand to touch and draw Yolande to him; with his bodily arms he might enfold her body; but inasmuch as a certain fact known to him and not to her debarred him from marrying her, this semblance of possession in time and space must be bought at no less a price than separation in eternity. Love and immortality would slip from his grasp, and only lust and death remain in it.

This high and vital insight wrought upon its subject but a transient effect. To have been capable of it attested spiritual refinement; but he had so conducted his life as to straiten its loftier capacities, and the instincts of a lower range of feeling followed hard upon the shining footprints of the pure intuition.

The senses do not argue; they wield a power beyond logic. Awakened and warmed, their voice is but an inarticulate cry for fruition, come what may! Yolande was so near; her sphere so wooed him; the sweet intent of her heart was so contagious; and the idea of never—never, for one instant!—

yielding to its invitation was so intolerable that his blood leaped up in mutiny. Oh, to kiss her once—no more!

No sooner had the conception of this kiss entered into him than he knew, in the marrow of his nature, that its reality was at hand; and the flash of that conviction lit up for a moment the scenery of abrupt summits and abysses, amidst which his spirit now walked. But he no longer wished to see his moral environment; it had lost its significance for him. He would focus himself upon Yolande.

Yet was he obscurely aware of a moral revolution accomplishing in himself, closing the upward channels of influx, and throwing wide those that opened downward. He did not regret it; it left him at his ease. Temptation—the interior combat of good against evil—tortures only while it lasts; the issue, whichever side it favor, brings repose and delight, since the man is then identified with (as the case may be) the angel or the devil.

Meanwhile he was heedful to flatter the susceptibilities of his gentle nurture and love of comely seeming by ignoring as yet the more sinister biddings of his new master. To kiss her once—once in the lapse of a lifetime to have verified the reality of mutual passion—was this yielding too much to the frailty of poor human nature? One sad, delicious kiss of love and of farewell combined—it was little enough to claim. Nay, it was a right due himself and her, to disallow which were vain hypocrisy. From the ends of the earth they two had met and loved; they must part—so be it; but not without exchanging a pledge which should serve to banish doubt and assure them of reunion hereafter.

Enough of justification! the delight of the expectant senses, rushing up from below into his brain, inundated with its impatient flood the feeble barriers of conscience. But he was not a man of the world for nothing; he knew the value of restraint in sensu-

ality. An untried youth would have sprung
at once to consummation, but Strathspey,
warily voluptuous, would steal upon gratification, missing not a throb of the kindling
senses, savoring every relish of pleasure.
When the culmination came it should have
suffered qualification in none of the preceding stages.

So swift is the mind the pregnant inflec-
tion lent to her last word by Yolande had
scarce ceased to vibrate in his ears before his
response was determined.

"You can't understand loneliness," he
said, "because you've never known what it
is to feel that you are all want, and that
some other inaccessible person is all fulness. Nor had I till I saw you, though I
had been lonely enough! But I recollect
in some nursery tale about the man who
didn't believe in fairy-land, and got on
very well with his scepticism until he met a
person who knew the way there; and she—
meaning him a kindness—gave him just one

glimpse of the enchanted kingdom. From that day he was a lost soul, wandering about in blind and hopeless quest of a good and beauty not created for him, which he had better never have . . . No!" he broke off, letting fall the threadbare cloak of his fable and rising impetuously to his feet, while his voice sank and grew husky, "I won't say that. I am better off for having met you. It's worth a thousand such lives as mine to have seen and known you as I have to-night!"

She had turned her face fairly towards him, and remained with head erect and eyes full opened, as the Egyptian lioness sits in stone. Now she also rose, with a slow and stately movement, and confronted him.

But it was so long before she spoke that he began to fear he had miscalculated, and fallen into the crude error of over-confidence. He had expected a tremulous and faltering agitation, amidst which he would

move to his goal as with the self-mistrust-
ful grace of one protesting his unworthiness.
He felt mistrustful in good earnest now,
and bit his lip; was it possible he had made
himself ridiculous?

It was Yolande's greatness of soul he had
failed to gauge. Her silence was the pause
of a reverent and noble nature on the threshold of voluntary and irrevocable change.
Her princely heart harbored no doubts of
the man she loved. As for his reference
to the "inaccessible," she thought he meant
no more than the old chivalric illusion—the
knight never worthy in his own eyes of the
guerdon of his lady's favor. Her guileless
honesty endowed him with scruples more
generous than he had ingenuity to frame;
and she sought so to make the gift of herself to him that the true benefactor should
seem to be himself.

At last she said, "That enchanted kingdom—if you care to be its king—" and
stopped, feeling that no parable, however

graceful, was of dignity worthily to bear her simple meaning.

She slightly raised her arms, with the palms of her hands towards him, and said, in a voice like the murmur of a distant bell,

"If you care for me, I am yours."

VII

"Me would the Dragon slay—
Shield, Spear flung I away!
A Holy Dove I came—
He burned in his own Flame!"

THERE is a moment when to the pure in heart this seeming amorphous and unwieldy universe (sprawling yonder beyond Arcturus and nebular spirals, and here vanishing again, despite help of lenses, in infinite microscopic perspectives) suddenly, obedient to the omnipotent vibration of an inspired heart, slips from behind the rigid screen of the letter, and appears transfigured, a spirit divinely human, of substance and form correspondent with angelic love and wisdom, and acknowledging a true infinity in the eternal instant of a lover's kiss.

Into the tremulous passion of that marriage of melting lips flow all tender meanings and potent harmonies inhabiting and
sustaining the exquisite hypocrisy of nature.
It solves the riddle of the Sphinx, sunder-
ing with its gossamer touch the adamantine
bonds of time and space, and irradiating
with immortal human light the alien ob-
scurities of mortality. All the laborious
languages of the world and the literatures
which embody them convey no significance
more vital than is disclosed in this inarticulate greeting of sex to sex.

Yolande felt herself taken and held; during a breath or two something apart from
her will delayed her yielding; she seemed
traversing distances immeasurable, weighted
and yet winged with awe and wonder, as at
passing from the dim womb of dreams to
naked, dazzling, palpitating life. But she
was drawn onward; her bosom must im-
press its softness upon the firm strength of
his body; she saw his face nearer to hers

than seemed credible—too near to be discerned, save as a dark, overshadowing, indrawing power. Her eyelids involuntarily fell, that she might behold the invisible: then came the apocalyptic touch! A message of vital flame, scarce known upon the lips ere tingling couriers had borne it to all regions of her being, near and far; welding to the male the female fibres of her life, and changing her from maid to woman. She felt the masculine more intimately hers than aught of her own had ever been; and saw, in instantaneous vision, her very self in him. The creative mystery, simple as sublime, was unveiled to her illuminated soul, and showed her, in human marriage, but reunion of the parts of a divinely planned antecedent whole.

Meanwhile the agent of her spiritual increase was, for his own part, already entering the shadows of torment.

At that moment of the embrace the perfume of the orange-blossom, idly plucked in

the garden while he was still a man, had
stolen to his nostrils, and summoned from
the past a scene in which the original of the
cloud-sculptured countenance had borne a
part with him. His heart rose in hate
against it, but was powerless to dissipate the
image of that smiling malice; it moulded
itself as a mask over the pure features of
Yolande, and its curling lips seemed even
to intercept the kiss for the sake of which
he was abdicating honor. It turned to bitterness and confusion the sensual ecstasies
for which he had bargained, yet forced him
to feign enthusiasm, lest this new-crowned
young queen of love suspect his fealty. He
had marred his delight and lost her, for she
was rapt out of his reach by that very joy
which transfigured her in conjoining her to
the lover whom she deemed him to be. In
the Paradise whose gates he had opened to
her he himself could have no share: those
gates had closed upon her, and his way was
barred by the flaming swords of the cher-

4

ubim.   Yet must he play out the rôle, and
profess to pace by her side along the thymy
paths, while in truth he was gnashing his
teeth unknown and unpitied in the outer
darkness.

But this was intolerable. If there were no
means of getting where she was, might he
not nevertheless draw her back to himself?
She was but human, after all!

As this question insinuated itself within
him, the answer, like a serpent, wriggled
across his mind, and was hidden again in
obscurity of its own engendering. But he
did not miss the hint of the crawling base-
ness.   The snake which had dragged down
stainless Eve from her high estate lurked in
Eden still, ever alert to repeat the eternal
infamy.   Yolande loved and trusted him:
her trust could be betrayed, her love corrupted, and she herself — or what was left
of her—become the testimony of his triumph.

When a man voluntarily cuts loose from

good he plunges into hell headforemost.
The higher degrees of his nature are the first
to be depraved.   But his evil harmony with
himself endows him with a temporary power.
Strathspey's eyes brightened; his faltering
nerves were restrung; he met Yolande's gaze
firmly, and scrupled not to peer deep into
that shadowy translucence.   It was pretty to
prattle of angels; but here in his arms, her
pliant body undulating in touch with his,
was a breathing feminine temptation, whose
fragrant lips of flesh and humid, gleaming
eyes called for anything but abstractions and
moralities.   It was well to set bounds beforehand; but human nature, once aroused, takes
things into its own hands, and carries them to
their natural consummation. He had thought
to end with a kiss; perhaps he might; he
had at any rate begun with one.

What man, fairly tempted, had ever finally prevailed against temptation? The temptation might be inadequate, the subject lack
virile integrity, or opportunity fail; but to

be tempted was to yield, since only those ripe to succumb were open to the lure.

Thus reassured, Strathspey, his lips against hers, muttered through his teeth, " My darling ! can it be true?   You love me !"

The words, despite their good intrinsic quality, rang false in his own ears: it being the misfortune of the sensual counterpart of love to vulgarize whatsoever it touches. True love, forever unprecedented, imparts its freshness to its instruments, and the dullest commonplace in word or act comes from it crowned with rarity: for the source is divine and infinite.   But the other passion, emanating from the corporeal degree of selfhood, inevitably repeats its one base note in every deliverance, and infects with its essential staleness the most noble phrase or gesture.   It cannot be helped; the fruit of profanations, if sweet on the tongue, is bitter in the belly, and fatal withal to life.   Its votaries have their reward.

But if that old serpent still crawls in Eden,

the Divine Humanity, in these days, also abides there; and the pure-hearted are environed with its sphere, the effect whereof is either to avert evil communications or to transform them into good. Yolande perceived nothing of the harm which threatened her.

With a gesture modest as impassioned she laid her sweet palms upon his face and pushed him away from her.

"Let me go—I want to think!" she said, breathless and rosy, a smile shining through tear-drops in her eyes. "Oh, you have kissed me, sir!—No: we must be apart a little."

"We've been too much apart already: come!"

But she drew back a step, breathing deep, and looking at him with a tender wonder. He could not follow her moods; but this seemed like coquetry. The male brutality latent in him began to bristle through the suavity of training.

"Yolande!"

She kissed her white hand to him and courtesied. " Mr. Strathspey!"

"Are you laughing at me? Don't call me that!" he exclaimed, roughly, angrily conscious of being worsted in this encounter.

She seemed scarcely to hear him. She turned from him, and looked out across the valley, fetching a long, delectable sigh, and lifting her white chin, while her fingers wandered over the delicate hair at her temples.

" Let me think!" she repeated, in an inward voice. " We must be in order now—like the other angels! Oh, what a plunge—from time to eternity! Is the world where we left it?" She glanced upward. " There is the moon!"

The moon! Strathspey frowned and reddened; he was letting himself be made absurd. This delicious incoherence of Yolande —the bewilderment of a soul apotheosized at the amazing accost of love—appeared to his debased intelligence as nothing more than coquettish affectation. He would put an end to it!

He stepped forward, caught her hand, and
kissed it violently. Contrary to his expec-
tation, she did not resist, but permitted him
his will with it.

"Listen to me, sweet!" he said, with a
clumsy utterance. "Your people may be
back here any moment. What's the good of
acting like this? We are wasting our opportunity—"

At that point his unchained eyes, roving
here and there, were arrested by hers, in
which was dawning a mysterious, inner
smile. This so disconcerted him that he
dropped her hand and flung himself upon
the bench. He planted his elbows on his
knees, gripped his hands together, and bent
down his head.

"Do you play with a man who loves
you?" he growled.

She made no answer, but he felt her seat
herself beside him, so close that the white
film of her skirt drifted over his thigh. She
leaned nearer yet, but he did not move un-

til her silence constrained him sullenly to turn towards her.

A murmur of laughter, low and sweet, came brook-like from her throat and broke in aerial waves over his heated senses. The serpent in him, striving to hold its own, writhed outrageously for an instant; but its infernal life was quelled by Yolande's look of clear light and living fire, and it subsided out of sight. Strathspey, who had identified its evil being with his own, was by its defection left wellnigh exanimate: he sat, dulled and cold, all vigor gone out of him.

But through his stupidness penetrated the bell-like music of Yolande's voice, in which passion and innocence chimed as one. The ripple of tender mirth was gone, leaving a tremulous solemnity.

"You make me think that I know love better than you. I gave myself to you, and—you took me!" She paused, breathing more quickly. "You made me see and feel—" Her voice failed; she covered her eyes with her hands, presently adding, in a deep whisper, "I cannot say it!"

A huge moth, black as night, appeared and hovered before one of the trumpet-blossoms of the white stephanotis that clambered up a pillar of the veranda. So noiseless was the whir of its dusky wings it seemed a phantom. After peering awhile into the depths of the flower it suddenly vanished, as if annihilated where it hung.

"God gave us this," Yolande went on, folding her hands and drawing them in upon her bosom. "He sent us to each other — not for an hour, or for a lifetime, but forever — to love each other forever! Opportunity!"

Strathspey flinched inwardly at the accent of divine scorn which she threw into that word. But the unconscious irony of her entire view of their relation suffocated him. He said, with difficulty, "Have some mercy for flesh and blood!"

Her hand went forth with a princely movement and rested upon his. What vital warmth was in her touch!

"Since I am yours, so is my body with me," she said. "You are to love it for my sake. And I so love yours"—her fingers involuntarily tightened their grasp—"that I almost fear to forget that it is only the servant of my lover—his messenger: to forget Arthur for Lancelot!"

The clear serenity of her speech was checked by an incoming tide of troubled thought. Some repugnant agitation wrought and grew within her. All at once she rose to her feet, panting and pale.

"Don't let it come between us!" she exclaimed in a changed voice, which rose and fell turbulently. "Unless we hold to our highest we shall lose each other! We would better die now than bury ourselves alive in that dungeon! . . . Oh, never honor this clumsy, lying image of me more than me! I could never forgive you! I am jealous of

its lips and arms! If they should steal you
from me—or yours rob me of you . . ."

The ominous intonation of her voice, as
of a sibyl's denouncing judgment, abruptly
stopped, as though its limit of faculty were
reached. She was standing erect as a Greek
pillar, her hands clinched by her sides, and
all the storm of her emotion glooming and
lightening in her eyes. Strathspey, who was
also on his feet, stared and blinked before
her. She was herself the cherub with the
flaming sword!

She moved towards him. His nerves con-
tracted, as at the threat of a thunderbolt;
the flash of that mystic sword seemed poised
against his actual life. Her face seemed like
that of a spirit disincarnate, owning no kin-
dred with mortality. She gazed into him
and said, in a slow, fierce whisper,

"I could be terrible!"

And then, ere he could catch his breath,
came another change, sudden and over-
whelming. Her arms were about his neck,

her cheek against his, he felt the beating of her heart, and heard her voice thrilling in his ear, " I love you—oh, how I love you !"

She was incarnate once more: body and soul she was his. What he had desired had come to pass. But he could no more avail himself of her self-surrender than dead time can absorb living eternity. He was as a heap of embers whose smoky flicker has been dazzled out of existence by the noon-day sun. She was burning and throbbing in his arms, but his dry lips could scarce return her ambrosial kiss. Because he had coveted her unchastely the heavenly gift of chaste enjoyment was gone.

But through this impassivity of sense an obligation began to define itself, which brought with it a minor life of its own. Yolande had entered upon the delight of her kingdom: whatever atom of true manhood remained in him should be devoted to maintaining to the last her faith in its integrity. It was his duty to enact, with what

animation and illusion he might, the character of the lover competent to such a love as
hers — high-minded, reverent, ardent, pure.
For this passing hour he must shield her
from any shadow or chill of disappointment
or misgiving. So much was clear. But how
of the time to come? If to-morrow she detected his unreality, what would it profit her
to have believed in him to-day?

"I must disappear," he said to himself.
"She must believe I'm dead. She can stand
that better than finding me out. Her faith
in immortality will console her with the idea
that we shall meet hereafter. And I suppose the resources of the Celestial City can
provide for her, when she goes there, some
fellow such as she fancies I am!"

And so — perhaps with a pang of transcendental jealousy of his angelic rival — Strathspey addressed himself to carry out the least
unworthy of the several impulses which had
moved him since he alighted at Yolande's
door.

VIII

"In Fire sought, I hide in Snow;
   Lost in Delight, am found in Pain;
Present, I fade; but wise men know
   O'er Leagues and Years I bloom amain!"

BUT he soon saw that his scheme of a pretended death would not serve his purpose.

The world nowadays is not large enough to play hide-and-seek in—the light of publicity spoils the game. Where could Strathspey go that Yolande might not find him? how furnish convincing proof of his decease? A dead body is convincing!

Something must be done. For here was Yolande coming to her own — the woman new-created entering on the life she was made for—the young queen of love ascending her throne—and it was all a deception,

her kingdom an hallucination, and the ex-
haustless spring of passion in her must waste
itself upon a void. This was a tragedy to
touch the most indifferent. There was but
one way to mitigate it, and that was by dint
of another tragedy whose *dramatis persona*
should be himself. In plain terms, in order
to keep her faith in his honor, he must kill
himself.

"That sounds rather extravagant, though,"
he said to himself.

But the more he looked at the idea the
better he was pleased with it. The truth
was, he was in the temper for suicide, and
therefore prone to accept a pretext. It
seemed to him that a man prepared to die
for the sake of upholding a girl's ideal was
entitled to some respect. His manhood re-
asserted itself. He felt able to look her in
the face without shrinking. The shadow of
death purified and strengthened him. He
suddenly felt cheerful, and able to play the
light-hearted lover.

They were now pacing up and down the
stone pavement of the veranda. Yolande's
step was buoyant, and as they walked arm-
in-arm, she ever and anon turned and kissed
his shoulder. They moved as one, but their
thoughts were as disparted as zenith from
nadir.

" I didn't know how to manage so much
joy at first," remarked Yolande. " I was
caught up to heaven, and couldn't find my
way back. I wanted to give you more than
can be given—on earth at least. Our bodies
frightened me; but now I thank God for
them. They will teach how to love—all the
ways and wisdom of it. By trying to make
ourselves one flesh here we shall learn how
to be one angel afterwards!"

" Don't you think you'll ever get tired of
me, Yolande?"

" Tired of you! If eternity were a moment shorter than it is I should die of thirst
and hunger for you, beloved!—Stop!"
They paused, and she lifted up her face to

him. "I want you to kiss me—a slow kiss. Now I will tell you down into your heart I love you—love you—forever! Ah! did your heart hear it?"

She drew back her mouth from his, and they looked at each other.

No; assuredly the world was not large enough to hold him and her apart from each other; it must be death.

They resumed their walk. She tossed her head, and threw a kiss from her finger-tips to the stars.

"Do you think me beautiful?"

"All the good and beauty of the world are promises which you have fulfilled."

She breathed this in, and grew yet lovelier.

"That proves I belong to you. The more and the longer I am yours the more beautiful shall I become. For my beauty is made by your seeing it, and your eyes were made to see it, and no other. Ah, beloved, I pray I may fulfil for you the promises

5

of the world.   But see, how beautiful they are !"

Indeed, the night was exquisite almost beyond the reach of sense to apprehend it. On the south the sky-line was fringed by the feathered fronds of a row of palms; their surfaces faintly glistened in the moonbeams, and they gave forth in the breeze a delicate hissing sound, like pattering raindrops. The moon was a goddess effulgent, wellnigh too fair for mortal gaze; she had dissolved both upper and lower clouds, yet but few stars were strong enough to penetrate the mantle of her light; the largest of them rested just on the peak of one of the northeastern mountains, and might have been mistaken for an earthly fire; but as our dark planet rolled towards the east the mountain sank and left the bright star ascendant.

The firmament itself was dark and yet luminous—warp and woof of a myriad delicious hues. Threads of purple and azure were interwoven with gold and crimson, depth beyond depth, splendor within splendor, subdued into a lucid harmony of shadow. But ah, that marvellous crescent! not white, nor yet golden, but the ineffable counterpart of the dark; her glory was as that of immortal eyes, kindled by such passion as immortals feel—a dissolving brightness, a lustre of celestial wisdom inspired by celestial love. She was not aloof from the beholder, but blended herself with his soul, identifying herself with his emotion, and illuminating his thought. To the inner sense that abyss of frozen and lifeless space that parted her sphere from ours had no reality. She lived within the heart; she was the language of the night—the key that unlocked its meanings and uplifted them to harmony.

There were silent motions and elfin sounds in the air round about. A great white owl feathered its soft flight over the tree-tops, passing fleetly from visibility to invisibility; and the tender, greenish sparkle of countless fireflies throbbed far and near, lanterns of frolic fairies. Insects and tree-toads chirped and sang unseen, maintaining an interior palpitation of sound that was so multitudinous as to seem rhythmical; and ever and anon, distinct above the diapason, yet uniting with it, came the croak of a gecko, crawling concealed near by, and answered by another at a distance. All the minute life of the earth was vocal and active, but man and the larger animals were still.

"So the world has been from the beginning, and so it will always be," said Yolande. "But my face will become old and wrinkled, and this body of mine bent and infirm. For we shall live many, many years together on earth—shall we not, my beloved?—for we are both of us full of strength and health."

He drew a long breath. "You ought to outlive me; you are scarce twenty, and I am thirty-seven."

Three days was the limit he had given himself to settle his affairs and step out of this life.

" No; how could I live after you had left
me? God gives us our life every moment;
but when a man and woman have been made
one she must receive her life through his.
No, I shall go first; then you will not
have the sorrow of dying and leaving me
alone."

Strathspey laughed a little. " Barring accidents, then, let us leave it so." He saw, in
his mind, high above the mountain river that
flowed between his house and hers, a bridge,
narrow, with a low parapet. Just beyond
the road made a sudden turn. A horseman,
galloping down the declivity, and forgetting
what lay on the other side of the turn, would
go headlong over into the gulf.

His hand lay upon the marble railing.
Yolande leaned forward and rested her
smooth cheek upon it. They had resumed
their bench.

" I shall be glad of that ugly mask of old
age," she said, " put on us just when experience has confirmed our faith that only im-

mortal love and beauty can be real. Instead of hindering, it will help us see each other as we are. And we shall get so used to disregarding what only seems, that when our eyes open in Paradise we shall say to each other, 'You have not changed!'"

"Suppose I were to go first, Yolande, do you think you would know if my spirit came to you and said, 'It is all right: I am alive, and I love you?'"

"How could I help knowing?" she returned, gravely.

He stooped, and kissed the tender, white region underneath her ear. She sighed with pleasure.

"How infinite happiness is!" she murmured. "How can I hold so much? And yet to-morrow I shall be happier, and happier still the next day, and so on forever. My beloved, there are people who are sick, or starving, or miserable in some way — husbands and wives who do not love one another. You might almost think unhappiness too was infinite. If we could only comfort them !"

"We must first become better acquainted with our own happiness," replied Strathspey.

That rider had plunged thirty feet down to the rocky bed of the torrent. Upon consideration, however, he had first dismounted. There was no reason for making the innocent animal an accomplice, and Strathspey was very fond of his horse. It would be thought he had been thrown.

"Yes, you are right," said Yolande, looking up with a smile. "I don't know myself yet—my new self." She suddenly added, "You must introduce me to her—your wife —to Mrs. Strathspey."

He stared at her, the blood thundering in his heart, his lungs empty of air. She seemed to darken and quiver out of sight: in her place emerged that fair phantom of mocking malice; . . . it withdrew, as voluntary thought and comprehension returned to him. There sat Yolande, perplexed and a

little troubled, peering through the shadow
that was mercifully on his face.

She put her hand on her bosom. "Something — something cold went through me
here!" she said. "Did you feel it too?"

He nodded—speak he could not.

She shivered and then laughed. "We
already feel each other's feelings—soon, perhaps, we shall think each other's thoughts.
Look in my eyes and see!"

But he bent his face down. After a moment he felt her soft fingers pass caressing-
ly through his hair.

"What is it, beloved?" she asked.

The touch and quiet voice restored him.

"I'm not fit to read your soul nor to
have you read mine," he said, speaking
huskily from a dry throat. "I wish I could
shut a door between to-night and all I've
been or done before—"

He checked himself, fearing to have said
too much; but Yolande, in her proud humility, was above suspicions.

"Yes, you're wiser than I," she said. "A rose doesn't look back to when it was a bud; and God will take care of me to-morrow— to-night is enough for us. But to be your wife—you must help me realize that! And you might begin by asking me to marry you, sir. Do you know you haven't done that yet?"

He made an attempt to echo her playful tone.

"I'm not in a ceremonious enough vein to-night. At our next meeting I'll submit the proposition with all the honors."

The body had been swept down through the wild falls and eddies of the river, and cast up on a little bank of sand below the bridge. A group of persons were looking at it.

"And then," she went on, "you must let me know your first name, too. You were angry with me a little while ago because I called you 'Mr. Strathspey.' But what else could I?—look at this."

She pulled at a silken cord round her neck and drew from its hiding-place in her bosom a man's visiting-card bearing the legend " Mr. A. H. Strathspey."

" There, you see—" she began ; but her voice faltered and a blush spread over her face and neck. " I never thought I should show you that."

Tears came to Strathspey's eyes at this revelation. It seemed to bind them together as nothing else had done. She had loved him from the beginning, in the sacredness of her maiden privacy, before knowing whether he loved her. His heart melted within him for tenderness and humility.

" God bless you, Yolande !" said he. " Will you let me keep this now? It is—it—will do me more good than you can imagine."

She slipped the silken cord over her head, kissed the card, and then passed the loop round her lover's neck. With her arms on his shoulders and her mouth at his ear she whispered, "There's only one thing in the world I would exchange for it—and that is —you! So now you are my own!"

"I am your knight; this is your favor which I wear in my fight with the dragon. If he were Death himself I shouldn't be afraid of him now. If he gets the better of me, bury me with this on my heart." He looked at her with sparkling eyes.

She shook her head and pressed her arms against her sides with a tremor.

"Don't jest about death, beloved; it has its dark side, after all, though till now I never felt it. But every moment and every way of you are so dear to me that I fear any change. You didn't tell me your name; what does 'A. H.' stand for?"

"Angus—Angus Hugh; there's no secret about it. But I want you to call me only by the name you gave me to-night; no one else has ever called me that. Call me only 'Beloved.'"

"Oh, but I can call you both! And those

are lovely names; they fit into my heart and mouth. Listen, Ang—"

" Don't—don't!" he said, muffling her lips with his. " Any one can call me by those names, and I have heard them from people I hate and that hate me. Don't put yourself with them!"

Yolande smiled in scorn.

" As if any one who knew you could hate you! Besides, I would make you forget all the others and remember only me. Well, since you're so foolish, it shall be as you wish; but only for to-night! to-morrow—"

" By-the-way," he interrupted, with an air of recollecting himself, " to-morrow — for the next two days, in fact—I sha'n't be able to come here. There are some affairs I have to attend to at once. After that I shall be free."

Yolande's dark eyes dilated, and the corners of her mouth drooped. " To-morrow — two days!" she repeated, in an almost inaudible voice. " Three days — for

you won't come till the third afternoon.
Oh, I can't—"

"After that I shall be free," he said again.

There was a silence. Yolande looked away
towards the mountains.

"This is Tuesday. Wednesday — Thursday — at what time on Friday will you
come?"

Strathspey hesitated. An idea struck
him. Could a disembodied soul appear to
one in the flesh? In time past he had half
believed so. She had said that she would
know if his spirit visited her. They loved
each other, and love brings spirits together.

"On Friday, before sunset," he said at
last, "I will be with you."

It was a weird promise, and a chill trickled
through his nerves and about the roots of
his hair as he gave it. But he meant to
keep the appointment.

"Now, if you don't come — " she began,
threateningly. She did not finish her sen-
tence. A plan to surprise him had suddenly

occurred to her. She smiled, and nodded mysteriously.

Meanwhile Strathspey had been continuing his speculations. His brows expanded and his heart beat stronger.

If love brought spirits together — if he could consciously approach Yolande after death—then why might not their conjunction become permanent? The philosophy of such matters was beyond him, but the inference seemed logical. The veil between the two states of being might often be drawn; but what of that, if they could be assured of the reality of their intercourse? And there would be no bar to their union, since his death would have removed it. The conception affected him like the rising of the sun at midnight.

He cast a glance back over the development of his relation with Yolande. At first idly attracted by her beauty, he had been gradually won by glimpses of the depth and rarity of her nature, but, knowing the hidden

helplessness of his position, he had put away
the thought of love. To-night, caught unawares by passion, he had arrived at the
pass whence only a treacherous crime or the
escape of death could rescue him. Each of
these had seemed to imply separation from
Yolande. But now he saw in the latter a
possible tie more intimate than he could
otherwise hope to compass.

Doubtless, in his passion and ignorance,
he was counting on a possibility which a far
profounder and cooler man might have re-
jected. But Providence willingly adapts itself to human error, and makes it the parent
of good. A mistaken hope may set us on an
upward path that had else been missed, and
each effort supplies strength for the next.

"I will come, and never after leave you,"
Strathspey repeated. "I shall be free."

They stood up and faced each other. It
was best to go now while the glow of faith
was still vigorous.

"It would be buying even our farewell

minutes too dear to wait till we must part before others," said he, with a smile.

"We cannot part," murmured she, inclining towards him like a wave about to break. "I go with you, beloved — I stay with you. If you want to find me, search the marrow of your bones and the core of your heart, for I am there! Go now, so that I may begin to be with you. Go, or this body of mine will stifle me!" She broke off with a laugh more touching than tears.

Her vehemence startled him; it was as if she had guessed his purpose. With a touch of heroism he said, "Only three days more, you know—less than three!"

She took his face between her hands and looked at him.

"Thought and hope are the part of love which only absence can give," she said, at length. "Now I know how pain can be happiness." She closed her eyes with those words, and when she opened them again her lover was gone.

IX

"From Death's Beleaguer Life besieged I shield—
Inmost from outer guard, Pure from Impure :
My sacred Infant fain would Cowards yield
To Age profane, stood not my Name secure !"

STRATHSPEY mounted his horse and rode down through the gate, and out into the road towards the wood. The level moon-rays shone upon him as he rode. He did not look back.

Three days more of earth ! He drew a full breath, struck his clinched hand against his chest, twisted his mustaches. He touched his horse with the spur, reining him in at the same moment, and felt him bound beneath him. He heard the steel-shod hoofs smite the solid road. Only three days more ! Life, life, life !—what is it ?

Now that the end (or the change) was so

6

near, he could contemplate the scope and proportions of his career, as might a biographer hereafter. A bright, happy, active beginning; a young manhood blooming with lusty potencies, practical capacities, clean ambitions; honor from man and favor from woman; the world all running his way, bearing him on and up; then, to crown good fortune, a brilliant marriage. After that, seven years of bitter, stubborn, degrading antagonism — the more bitter because hidden from the world — and finally, surrender of hope, and decorous separation by mutual consent.

That was the story. She had ruined him, by the only means that can ruin such a man; sapping the sources of his energy, destroying the roots of his self-respect, stabbing the vitals of his aspiration. She knew where to strike. She had fathomed the frailties of the strong man, and practised, with fatal sagacity, the art of inflaming his evil and blighting his good. But was not he also to blame?

'Twas very likely. Now that the sands were
run out, he might judge dispassionately,
making all allowances for her, and sparing
no truths against himself.

He rode into the wood; it was dark, save
for the web of tangled fire which the fireflies wove around him. Upon the canvas
of the night he saw her in all her phases
from first to last. Her image had been so
branded into him that at times of strong
emotion it rose into visibility, like the mark
on the shoulder of a convict when struck
with the hand. She was a fascinating creature, carrying her gifts of intellect, wit, and
beauty, and her refinement of wealthy breed-
ing, with a grace as light as a child's bearing
a handful of wild-flowers. In whatever society she found herself, she became the spark
of vitality, the point of high light.

Oh, that slender, vivid face; that airy figure; those delicate lips of subtle laughter
and elfin satire; those dancing, glancing,
measuring, probing eyes! But within were

the intrepidity of a trooper, the cruelty of a
Borgia, the malignity of a Mephistopheles—
such qualities, at least, he had found in her.
Yet he could admit that, united to another
than himself, she might have proved gracious and lovable. There are spiritual com-
binations whose parts, benign in themselves,
turn each other to poison by transcendental
chemistry. He and she who, apart, might
have been fountains of use and honor, had
by their union transformed each other into
powers of evil, and sowed in society yet one
seed more of the old corruption.

At times when she had been unconscious
of observation—when, perhaps, she had been
recalling girlish visions of what life might
have in store for her—he had seen her look
so wistful and tender that he could have
wept and loved her. But did he make overt
hints thereto, scepticism and aversion would
flicker from her eyes and curve her lips. "I
know you to the bottom, and you are despi-
cable," said her glance. Possibly she too had

at times tried to approach him, and he, blind
to her intent, had repulsed her. The move-
ments of their natures were mutually inscru-
table. Save in external ways, devoid of life,
they could not meet. Stars in their orbits
were not more alien than they; but whereas stars respected the decree of boundless
space, ordained to admit free development
of opposites, he and she had forsaken their
divinely appointed paths and swept into dis-
astrous collision.

Nevertheless, during seven years one roof
had covered from the world the unceasing
duel which was their existence. She sur-
passed him in vitality and constancy of hatred, and could draw delight from his suffering though her own might be not less; she
planned and brooded and sought new ways
of attack, cunningly and persistently pro-
voking his more passive aversion, until at
last it would kindle into flame, and then it
was terrible and pathetic to see her joy.

There was a period when he had thought

that her hate might perhaps be a sort of perverted love. In a sense, a woman who hates and she who loves are akin. Both feed on their passion, seek intimate ways to gratify it, and tempt its object to demonstrate a responsive feeling. Hate might then be construed as love driven by its intensity to mask as its own opposite. Was this the key to conduct which had often seemed to Strathspey insane in its malignity? Might not love, unable for whatever cause to find its normal expression, prompt to deeds of fantastic malice—nay, to murder? For murder would bind them together in a sort of infernal marriage; thereafter each fresh act of mutual rancor would weld their souls together more inextricably, till at last they should become, as it were, a single organism of agony, tearing continually at its own heart with a rage inexhaustibly renewed by what it thirsted to destroy.

But this supposition had not survived analysis. Were the antagonisms of selfhood as infinite as its attractions, the power of hell would equal that of heaven. But hell, owning the self-love of the finite creature as its source, partakes of the creature's finiteness, whereas heaven exists by love, the substance of the Infinite Creator. Hatreds die out in their own evil fire, while the vitality of love cannot but increase to eternity. And though love may at first attract with a force that reacts towards repulsion, yet the innate health and sanity of the divine emotion presently correct this perversity. Only sophistry can pretend a real confusion between the two.

But why should the coming together of these two—which at worst was hardly more than a venial mistake of judgment—involve penalties so severe? Crime expects punishment; but who would declare their marriage a crime? They had met, been attracted to each other, and their union had seemed, both from a personal and from a worldly point of view, expedient. Their previous lives had been blameless. With what justice, then, were they called on to suffer such torments? —the ill effects of which, far from being restricted to the immediate pain they wrought, darkened and corrupted the nature of their victims, and set them on the path leading to adultery and murder.

Such an arraignment of the divine goodness arises from our confounding the qualities of human with those of natural law.

Natural law (whether on the material or the spiritual plane) differs from human law in that it regards no persons and inflicts no chastisements. It is simply a beneficent current conservative of the integrity of the entire creation. Opposition, be it witting or unwitting, to this current implies for the opponent pain or annihilation, as the case may be. But the law itself never punishes— it can only bless.

Thus the saint who falls overboard is drowned despite his sanctity, since water misapplied could abdicate its asphyxiating quality only by violating the economy of the universe. Innocent of animosity against the saint, it yet kills him in deference to interests infinitely above those of his continued physical existence. Were water subject to human instead of to divine administration, no doubt it would drown sinners only, and let the elect go free.

Natural law, in short, being the guise assumed by Divine Love in its function towards organic or unconscious man, is out of relation with his personal or self-conscious phase — at least, until the latter shall have fulfilled its office of accomplishing the voluntary conjunction of creature with Creator. On the other hand, human law deals with the selfhood exclusively, attacking its illusions as realities, and treating sin (which is but the characteristic and transient insanity of the selfhood) as if it involved actual discord between the divine and the human nature. Justice and punishment are its shibboleths—brave words, but the ideas they express own no heavenly origin; earth begat them, and in the torrid swamps of hell they riot with tropic luxuriance. No taint of justice defiles Him who said, " Neither do I condemn thee!" nor does that father punish who welcomes his prodigal with kisses and feasting. Punishment lies in spontaneous recognition of our discord with infinite love, and repentance is seeking again that conjunction with life from which crime would divorce us.

But though human and natural law differ as do finite and infinite in both quality and function, we are yet often misled by the former's shallow pattern into striving to divert, by personal pleas of guilt and innocence, the cosmic sweep of the latter. Strathspey and his wife broke the natural law which would marry persons and things mutually compatible, and no others. Pain, which they interpreted as punishment, was the consequence; and being conscious of individual righteousness in their general relations with society, they deemed their fate unjust, and that they did well to be angry. Since no man convinced them of sin, why should God do so? Having rendered unto Cæsar the things that were Cæsar's, they held their debt to their Father as implicitly liquidated.

But their trespass transcended the limits of personal aberration; it was wrong done not to men, but to the nature of man, for which they—agents at once of the wrong and partakers of the nature—were bound to suffer. Not individual responsibility, but the integrity of creation was in question, which both in generals and in particulars is a marriage. Wisdom espouses love, form substance, man woman, all save the last being natural and therefore perfect unions; the last, spiritual as well as natural, because voluntary, may be profaned, and, instead of rising the radiant consummation of the rest, may sink below the naïve couplings of the brute.

Mismarriages, outcome of artificial culture and ideals, are against nature, which sponta-

neously rejects them. The misery they beget
seeks retaliation on its cause and compensation for itself, and murder embodies the first,
adultery the second impulse. Circumstance
and training may restrain much, but from the
moment husband and wife have looked on
each other with hatred the worst is possible.
And though society — so long as these victims of its ceremonial and their own egoism
abstain from overt criminality — continues
complacently to entertain them, yet the instant their evil emerges from the darkness
of their hearts into the light of vulgar publicity is a merciless leopard at their throats.
Hence hypocrisy completes the infernal cat-
egory. But the penalties of human law can
be avoided only by allowing those of natural
law the fuller scope.

All the ingenuity of intellect and wisdom
of experience have failed to devise a cure for
the predicament in which Strathspey and his
wife had placed themselves. Divorce restores
nothing that has been lost, and patient for-

bearance seems beyond the strength of those weak enough to fall into the snare. But if earthly resources offered no relief, there, once more, was death, and what might lie beyond. And for Strathspey death was now both relief and hope!

Riding out of the dark wood, he saw the mountain lifting itself sublime against the stars. The voice of the river, calling him, promising peace, came distinctly to his ears. As he breasted the ascent he spoke to his horse, which responded with a gallop. Higher they mounted and higher, into cooler air. Only three days more between him and freedom!

X

" Worlds, Wisdom, Power, the Sky, are thine by
    right,
Art thou so rich my suppliant to be.
Wouldst buy, base Mendicant, my wealth of me?
Hunger I sell thee, Nakedness, and Night!"

THE road, doubling in and out around
the projecting mountain-spurs, and
sometimes returning upon itself at a higher
level, gradually trended towards the east, to
the point where it crossed the river. On
either hand, as he rode, was a steep precipice, dropping darkly down on the right,
mounting sheer upward on the left, and
everywhere clothed with vegetation. The
tops of tall trees reached up as if to grasp
him from beneath, and the roots of others
overhung his head above. The pallid rib-
bon of road wound amidst this silent obscu-

rity like a path miraculously hung in space.
No breeze penetrated this mighty ravine;
each leaf and frond stood motionless as if
enchanted. But the vitality and profusion
of plant life were greater here than on the
lower levels; for the sharp summits of the
mountain caught the drifting clouds, and
compelled them to linger and dissolve in
constant showers, whence were begotten
thronging ferns and thick cushions and tap-
estries of moss. The leaves of the trees
spread larger, and the slender pillared boles
rose aloft as if in thronging competition for
the sky. Such fury of life, such immobility! Insects were fewer; the firefly showers
of the plain were reduced to here and there
a wandering atom of light; the chorus of
tree-frogs had dwindled to intermittent voices
of solitude. Only the rushing undertone of
the river abode unceasingly in the ear, rising
and falling as the road passed behind mountain parapets or surmounted them.

At length, half-way up the ravine, the

rider bore to the right and reached the narrow bridge. He halted on its arch, and
looked below.

Even since he had passed, that afternoon,
the stream had swollen. A tumult of waters hurtled downward, twisted and whirled
into fantastic forms, which from moment to
moment kept their contours unaltered — a
constant force casting in identical moulds
the ever-shifting substance, as soul moulds
body. Headlong motion thus assumed the
semblance of immobility, and the roar of the
cataract seemed disconnected with it — the
strain of a titanic harp smitten by the invisible spirit of the mountain. After Strathspey had gazed awhile, the vibration of this
mighty music communicated its contagion
to his brain, and he felt drawn as by a
myriad viewless but potent threads of be-
guilement to merge himself in the wild diapason. But he sat still—his hour was not
yet come!

His three days were none too many for

winding up his account with the world. In
order to vanish with a plausible appearance
of unpremeditation, many things must be
premeditated. He must plan out for himself an imaginary future, and prepare data
to convince whom it might concern that he
had been anticipating an existence full of
activities. And he must provide against the
possibility that any associate of his former
career—she above all from whose fatal shadow he was escaping—should be induced to
reveal the facts that it behooved him to
hide. Until their union hereafter Yolande
must deem his honor spotless.

"And what then?" he asked himself. "In
the end a time will come when all hearts are
open and no secrets hid. She will know me
as I am at last. Then why not as well now
as later? Am I hiding the truth for her
sake, or for my own? Am I not a coward
both towards Yolande and towards my wife
— an out-and-out coward? Hum! I must
look into this."

7

In the preoccupation of his bent to suicide, its justification had not concerned him. It now became insistent, as if some one stood beside him and demanded an answer.

A coward deserting his colors under fire! The very eagerness with which he had accepted this facile means of shirking trouble should have warned him to doubt its honesty. It had taken a lifetime of error and selfishness to bring him to his present pass —what miraculous virtue lay in a plunge off a bridge to make wholesome and straighten his diseased and crooked soul? And since the soul gives the environment, this also—so far as its spiritual bearing on him went—must remain unmodified-by any act of mere physical violence. Nay, the unmuffling of the senses wrought by death would but make them more sensitive to the ills he sought to fly. He was not a coward, merely, but a fool!

"After killing myself I shall be as ill off as before, and probably worse," was his conclusion.

Then how could he expect to draw nearer Yolande by that act? Between pure and corrupt, selfish and unselfish, is a great gulf fixed, which might be bridged on the material plane, but not on the other. No; the only way to deserve Yolande was to cleanse himself from defilement—a process more laborious than drowning, and of a different character.

How should he be cleansed? Strathspey looked this way and that, but knew beforehand that there was for him but one course. He had desired death—he should have it; but death not of the body, but of mortal pride and egoism, involved in taking up again the burden he had laid down. He must take it up and so bear it that it at last be transfigured into the very robe and crown of salvation. Ah, that would be to die indeed! He groaned at the thought of it, and sweat started on his forehead.

"Can I do it?" he asked himself. "Go back to my wife and turn the curse of our life into a blessing? God! is there no other way?"

The temple we overthrew, and not another, must we rebuild. Marriage had been by him dishonored, and must by him be restored to honor. By what right otherwise might he claim its sanctification? Though between him and his wife no true conjugal union was or had ever been possible, yet might they too vindicate the holiness of its name. Their very disinclination to each other might render more pure and potent their loyalty to the marriage principle. No disguises! It must be understood that they came together in the teeth of personal impulse, to do impersonal right—their compensation, the austere satisfaction of atoning for wrong done to the human nature within them. Incompatible as individuals, as man and woman they could meet with respect and charity. They could educate each other to disregard surface discords of self for the sake of the vital harmonies within, and thus become fit for union beyond the grave with their true mates in the holy estate which they had forfeited here.

True, she might decline to co-operate in this enterprise. Easy to imagine the sarcastic scepticism with which she might greet the proposal. "You ask me to act as your moral disinfectant, to perfume you into the graces of another woman. You must excuse me! If she is too fastidious to take you as you are, she is perhaps better without you." But though at first she might hold that tone, Strathspey did not believe it would survive her recognition of his honesty. She was too intelligent to deny the truth of his argument, and, finding him practically faithful to it, would emulate his loyalty. In any event, his course must be the same. He owed her more reparation than she owed him ; his initiative had brought them together, and their separation had left her at the mercy of slanderous tongues, and to the temptation to take what solace lay in justifying their malice.

But by returning to the protection of her honor he would restore its value in her own eyes; and his self-effacement for ideal marriage' sake would, he hoped, reanimate her belief in it which their personal failure had slain. At any rate, he would do his best to rehabilitate her without and within.

So far, good; but what of Yolande?

His pretext for suicide had been to keep untouched her faith in him and her ignorance of worldly evil. The pretext—but was it the motive? Had he been unhampered, and another man with such a past as his had attempted to win Yolande from him, would he in that case have hesitated to disenchant her by the revelation of his rival's iniquities? Not he! he would have praised himself for warning her what a goodly outside falsehood hath. Plainly, then, he was seeking less to keep her from evil knowledge than to whitewash himself. But his duty to her was to be honest—to show her his seamy side, since he had one. It was not for him but for Prov-

idence to mould truth to ends of benefi-
cence. If it grieved or even alienated her, better that than to deceive her. She was like
other human beings, born into the world to
be shaped by knowledge and strengthened
by sorrow — not to slip through it in a vain
dream of its innocence. Knowledge of evil
is to the good the awakening of charity.
Heaven's light could not inform angels were
there no dark of hell from which to win re-
demption.

Strathspey looked down once more into
the foaming rapids and shook his head with
a short laugh.

"It's not so easy as I thought," said he.
"But have I got it in me to see this thing
through? Perhaps since I've been able to
see straight, I shall get strength to do right.
Well—don't grow cold on it! See her to-
morrow and tell her the facts day after to-
morrow—there's a steamer!"

He shook his rein and passed on up the
mountain.

XI

"When from Me thou strayest,
All Heaven thou betrayest.
So thou return to Me,
All Heaven shall wait on thee!"

DEAR ANGUS,— If you get this letter (there is just a doubt if I send it) you will know it is my last as well as my first, and requires no answer. It is a year since I saw you; I hated the sight of you then, and should still were you to return; but, as it is, I have no hard feeling towards you, and dare say that but for our marriage we might have been good friends. You are not a bad man, though I brought the bad out of you, and hated your good qualities because they were yours. Had you justified my hate by being an unmixed devil, I should have hated you less; but as I felt that hating you involved hating your good as well as your bad, and as that was injustice (which I hate), of course I hated you all the more.

"I could almost imagine a time or state in which

we could laugh at the absurdity of our marriage.
And yet a false marriage is throwing what is holy
to the dogs, which can never be laughable. Only
perfect love should possess what husband and wife
surrender to each other, and when there is no love
it is like dogs slavering over the communion-table.
It is about the only unmitigated tragedy I can
think of; for if the source of the stream be muddy,
how can anything pure ever come from it? Beside this misfortune our trumpery personal quar-
rel seems nothing. As fellow-sufferers we should
rather feel mutual sympathy and compassion. Any
injury we could do each other would be a trifle
compared with the injury already done us by our
marriage — a ridiculous anticlimax. One's sense
of humor must be low to admit of it. To curse
God and die (whatever that fine thing may be)
seems more dignified.

"The fact is, reason, which we so extol, never
fails to betray us at the pinch. Nothing is more
irrational than personal antagonisms. I might have
loved in another man the same things I hated in
you. What could be more silly? As if the same
wine poured into glasses of two different shapes
should in one be poison, in the other life! We call
it silly because it is a mystery beyond our compre-

hension. There seems to be something more potent (at least to our finite minds) in form than in
substance — perhaps because form itself is limita-
tion and substance infinity. Could you and I be
dissolved and the same material made up in other
forms, we might love each other. But forms can
never change, though their contents one hopes
may be purified. You and I could never, even were
we angels of the third heaven, endure each other's
presence. Luckily the universe has antipodes for
the accommodation of cases such as ours. Sirius
and Arcturus are both respectable stars, but nevertheless, I believe, are very remote one from the
other.

" I never told you, nor did you suspect it—but my
one supreme desire in this world was for a child. A
baby at my breast would have broken down the
hardness with which I protected myself against
you, and something precious in my heart would
have gushed out with my mother's milk. But now
I thank God no baby came, for evil and good would
have been so mingled in it that nothing could have
saved us. And since we were deprived of that
curse in guise of blessing, some real blessing may
await us hereafter. But I don't know exactly what
I mean by this. I can imagine no blessing fit to

name beside a dear little baby — my own precious baby—clinging to me and knowing nothing better than to love me. And that is an experience I can never have.

"I feel really sorry for you, and hope you can feel sorry for me. We wanted with all our hearts to be happy, and yet could not help being each other's misery. Love, I am convinced, is not a physical thing, but a spirit, without which the most beautiful physical conditions are an ugly corpse. To miss true love altogether may be death, but to try for it and miss it, as we did, is murder. You did me the irreparable harm of asking me to marry you, and I returned it by accepting you. We had fallen into the habit of patterning our conduct on what society did, and this seemed but the natural culmination of a thousand other dashing and shallow things; indeed, it was just that—the final step of a smoothly graduated series. But it was fatal as well as final: the devil leading us along in his fascinating way from one point to another, and at last, with his most insinuating grimace of all, pushing us over the precipice.

"Why should I say I forgive you, or that I ask you to forgive me? What is forgiveness? Seems to me all evil and all good are done through rather than by us; we but consent to be the medium. The account of mischief is even between us. We let ourselves be duped by that old charlatan of Genesis into accepting the flashy frescoes on the outer walls of the House of Life for the life itself within. He ogled you through my eyes and wheedled me through your voice. The masquerade was successful for the moment, threadbare though it seems now.

"I have had some idle time on my hands of late which I have occupied with meditations on your future. You have the masculine advantage of being able to weather such a storm as ours; and being in the prime of life, it would be against nature not to wish for a comfortable wife and a season of domestic felicity. It has been no hardship to me that our separation did not permit another marriage. I am deficient in the insatiable enterprise that animates some ladies in my position. But women's society of some kind is indispensable to most men. Now, I chose to believe—whether from vanity or from confidence in your self-respect—that so long as we lived under the same roof you allowed yourself no vulgar consolation. And though it may be assuming quite exceptional virtue on your part, I please myself with the thought that you have not done so even yet. I am jealous: not as a loving woman is jealous lest a rival win her man from her, nor as a dog in the manger, keeping from others what I need not myself. But I am jealous to be free from the reproach of having driven you to low actions, and to have you escape the degradation of doing them. For all its selfishness, this jealousy is the nearest approach to a wifely feeling (seems to me) I have ever had towards you. I want you to succeed despite our failure. And yet I confess that while we were together I did my utmost to defeat my desire by tormenting you past endurance. But a woman needs to feel she has some power over her husband, if only to make him hate her !

"But our separation put an end to this amusement, and I cooled down to a consideration of what was to happen to you. Had I had the enthusiastic temperament of a woman I read of in a French novel, I might have promoted your marriage by disinterestedly furnishing you with legal grounds of divorce. But my sense of humor would not allow of that. Barring that, there remained suicide; but, however little enamoured I may be of life, I have a distaste (as you know) for the sensational, and could not, besides, face the humiliation of leaving you to imagine that I died in despair at your abandonment. Moreover, I should have laughed in my own face in the looking-glass as I stood up in front of it to swallow my poison. In short, with every desire to help you out if I decently could, my ingenuity proved unequal to devise a means.

"But at this point circumstance intervened and enables me to close this long letter with a dramatic little surprise. The letter, by-the-way, has been even more tedious to write than to read. I have been a week at it, lying on my back, in such brief stints as my condition allowed. Have you been wondering what ailed my handwriting? My horse bolted in the park, and in spite of the heroism of two mounted policemen and my own groom, collided with poor old Mrs. Walsingham's victoria in the drive. My back was hurt (she escaped with a fright), and Dr. Jersey—you remember the pompous old goose coquetting with his reflection in the mirror while he made up his prescriptions—now sets me an outside limit of ten days. But I know myself, and what I want, and I don't think I shall keep them waiting more than five.

"This will be sent you immediately afterwards. I cordially congratulate myself, Angus, and you. I go to freedom, and I leave you free. It has been

neatly done, and, on the whole, promptly—for remember, some women in my place would have lin-
gered spitefully on to ninety. I am happy, and it
will be your own fault, now, if you are not. I send
you my best wishes, and beg you, as a last favor,
always to be polite to Mrs. Walsingham for my
sake.   VIVIEN STRATHSPEY.

"P.S.—I couldn't help putting that last in, just
for fun. I feel no bitterness, my dear boy, and I
hope there will be none in your thoughts of me.
                              "V. S."

Strathspey found this letter awaiting him
when he reached his house that night. He
read it, standing in his riding-dress at his
dressing-table, by the light of a candle ; then
he sat down and reread it, with many a
pause between the lines. As he finished it
for the second time, and the hand which
held the painfully pencil-written sheets sank
upon his knee, a little shower of rose petals
fluttered down and rested upon the signa-
ture of the dead woman, and upon the post-
script. They were petals of the rose which

Yolande had given him in the garden, telling him he would recognize it in heaven. It was as if the living had sent a message of sisterly tenderness to the dead.

Yolande and Vivien: the maid and the wife: the living and the dead: the beloved and the unloved! Yet were they sisters, one in sex, forms of one nature, gifted alike with beauty and mind and power. Why should a man love one and not the other, begetting misery and death where might be life and joy? In truth, as Vivien had said, this is a mystery of mysteries. Identical substance in differing shapes kindles here supreme desire, invincible repulsion there. Are human likes and dislikes but the mask of Divine Order, weaving the rainbow pattern of its web, tuning the flawless consonances of its symphony? Operating, like all creative power, through poles of kin and alien, innate and spontaneous in its subjects, and therefore unerring, order distributes like to like, and averts the disease of confusion. Only for Him to Whom naught save nothingness is alien are our finite differences indifferent; for He is the inmost of all and each, and in Him (albeit beyond our consciousness) abides our atonement.

"She was proud and generous," said Strathspey to himself, thinking thoughts too sad for the relief of tears. "She veils her death itself with raillery, so that I might not see my part in it. I left her to face the ruin of her life alone, and now she dies with a smile and a jest, so that I may the more easily be happy on her grave. For all her dauntless show of gayety and independence, her heart was broken. No one could heal it—I least of all, who wronged her most. No, nor the baby she longed for, since it would have been mine as well as hers. Yet she bore me no grudge; she desired a means to set me free, without even a legacy of remorse. Many a wife who talked more of love than Vivien of hate would have proved less unselfish in the end. Hers

8

is pure human kindness, found only in great souls. She humiliates me: even had we loved each other, she deserved a better man than I. And she asks me to think of her without bitterness! I wish she might have known what I had in mind to do. God has done best, no doubt; but had I been worthy, He would have let me be the means. What am I fit for, then?"

The most unflattering truth we are called on to acknowledge in this world is, that heaven, though it may be lost, cannot be earned.

XII

"Fires freeze without my Spark,
Where I shine not Suns are dark;
Wanting me, Life is but Death,
Heaven Hell but for my Breath."

STRATHSPEY folded up the rose
petals in the letter, and put both together in the envelope. He had no inclina-
tion to sleep; so having changed his dress,
he went out on the veranda, which com-
manded an outlook of many miles over
mountain, plain, and sea. A breeze came
whispering up from the east, and the air was
cool. It was near midnight.

But Strathspey was ill at ease. For the
second time since his parting with Yolande
were the foundations of the deep within him
broken up. He was thrown abroad in space,
without aim or orbit. To one used to sub-

sist on purposes, to pride himself on knowing his will and doing it, this uncertainty
was more trying than the execution of any
resolve, be it ever so arduous.

While he paced to and fro on the moun-
tain-top, his spirit tumbled far down in valleys of doubt and shame. The formless
darkness of the night corresponded with the
hollow gloom in his mind. The noise of
his foot-fall on the planks jarred upon his
nerves, and he halted and gazed out towards
the sea, though his eyes admonished him of
no outward objects. Silence and darkness!
Over him, as he stood, crept the sense of
solitude, isolation, rejection. He was alone
in the world and in the night, but still more
was he alone in the spirit. The departure
of Vivien seemed to separate him from all
the living world; even the image of Yolande
receded and faded like a dream; and God
Himself, as if holding him unworthy of so
much as chastisement, removed the last barrier to his desire, and turned away. In this

welter of despondence, familiar ideas became phantasmal; and almost the only thing remaining real was the fact of Vivien's death.

True, he had accounted her, living, the thorn in his side, the cloud before his sun, the clog on his aspiration; yet did her death leave him as a body deprived of weight, hanging impotent in the void. Even as his enemy (which she no longer was) she had been, in a sense, his only friend. For our apparent misfortune is often our surest link with our fellows; through discipline of darkness we learn to know and value light; and the fable of him who sold his shadow to the evil one betokens those who, seeking to shirk the common mortal heritage of ill, forfeit along with it their capacity for happiness.

Strathspey told himself that equity was not met in his case. Apparently nothing now withheld him from Yolande; but the appearance was a mockery. Debarred from atoning for his misdeeds, he was left incompetent to the freedom born of absolution. To qualify him for union with Yolande, he had relied upon a lifetime of self-abnegation with Vivien; but the latter being now impossible, with what face could he pretend to the former? Has not God forsaken him from whom He takes opportunity for amends? Nor is there comfort in the suggestion that, knowing his frailty, God wills to spare him the foredestined failure of an effort to atone. For above all things else a man prizes his liberty, since thereon depends his very being as a man; and will rather cling to it in the depths of hell than stand bereft of it beside the throne of the Almighty. Let him fail of virtue, if he must; let him sell heaven for a mess of pottage, if he will; but let not the Lord himself presume to tamper with his sacred freedom. And the man who believes himself to have been thus juggled with stands in peril of worse than death and the judgment.

A fierce resentment began to smoulder in Strathspey's heart. But he crushed it down, and tried to think again.

" What shall I do? Can I marry Yolande, revealing nothing? No: in the house of true marriage must be no locked chambers. Marriage must be free intercourse of her soul with mine—not a paltry game of hide-and-seek, leading us each year further apart. If I keep my true self from her, her true self will be lost to me ; my seven years taught me that, if nothing else. With Yolande and me, it must be all or nothing."

He stared intently into the darkness. Its very blankness made it plastic to the conceptions of fantasy, and his mind was unnaturally active. Something seemed to lurk yonder; no, only a throbbing in his own eyeballs, which seemed to—seemed to figure forth something—pshaw! He pressed his fingers over his eyes, and forcibly repressed the irregularity of his breathing. What had he been saying?

"Go to Yolande—that was the idea—go
to her and say, ' I have ruined one woman's
life ; reward me with yours !' She would do
it ; in her heavenly charity, she would accept
me. But how could I accept myself? My
sins are upon me ; ·no purgatorial fires have
burnt me clean ; I can show no guarantee of
good behavior. For aught I know or can
prove to the contrary, there may be an adul-
terer or a murderer here " — he struck his
clinched fist over his heart — " waiting to
practise on Yolande! No—I'll save her from
that, if I have to take myself by the throat
to do it ! If I could have purged myself—
a lifetime of sacrifice with Vivien — but
Providence, in its infinite wisdom, wouldn't
have that! I'm no good ; a lost soul, fit
only to be taken by the throat and—"

He checked himself, noticing that he was
speaking aloud, in a strange, excited voice.
A nervous shudder went through him ; then
another. He laid his hands upon the wood-
en rail of the veranda, bracing himself upon

it with all his force. It cracked; it broke, and a fragment of it came away. He flung it from him into the shrubbery, and wiped the sweat from his forehead.

"Come — mustn't get off your base, you know!" He laughed a moment between his set teeth. "A bit played out, my boy; but you're all right. Steady—as we used to say in the crew—steady!"

Suddenly he lifted his face and peered, ghastly pale, into the blankness of darkness beyond the veranda.

"Now, what the devil," muttered he, in the carefully restrained tone of a philosopher momentarily perplexed, "is that?"

Darkness and silence.

"Twenty - five years since that has happened to me," he went on, scarce audibly, and still maintaining his close gaze. "Used to see 'em after being ill; nervous organization, father said. It's nothing; only curious. What are you shuddering for, you fool?"

There was another pause.

" Old Maverick explained 'em to us in class at college. Images of external objects passing by the optic nerve to the brain are interpreted . . . That's the normal. But images may originate in the brain, which the optic nerve, unable to discriminate, reports back as also realities. There you have apparitions — subjective hallucinations. That's clear enough, I should think. I'll reason you down, damn you!"

The next instant he stiffened, his right arm stretched out tense as a harp - string, fingers extended. " Hold on !—just as you were, please! You can't move, you know, because—"

Gradually the tension relaxed, the arm fell, and the retained breath exhaled from the lungs. He nodded his head, and chuckled faintly.

" I knew I could reason it down. It's all right—only it had no business to move, because . . . What was it Maverick said ? No matter; bed and sleep are what I need. To-

morrow . . . Oh, you're *there*, are you?—
you scoundrel!"

He wheeled about and faced down the
veranda. It is horrible that such things are
permitted. Science and philosophy will lie,
and lie, and all the while the thing itself
creeps up behind you and frights the manhood out of you. Horrible!

And yet there was nothing ostensibly un-
pleasant in the figure confronting Strathspey. There were indeed some singular
points about it. Feature by feature and
limb by limb, it had a marvellously familiar
aspect; and despite the dense obscurity in
which it stood, it was visible in every detail.
But here one remarks another peculiarity—
that there were moments when it seemed
less distinct than at others. And these va-
riations were apparently dependent upon the
mental ebb and flow in the observer.

After all, however, since as we know every
man has two selves, what more natural than
that in seasons of special perspicacity they

should become objectively cognizant of each other?

"At all events, my dear fellow, here we are. No friend like a man's self to pull him out of a hole—and we are in a pretty deep one! But there's a way out—a clean, gentlemanly way—never fear!"

"That's my own voice — I'm saying all this!" Strathspey broke in. "Steady!"

He had a feeling that, by an effort, he might overcome and banish the figure; but how to put forth the effort he knew not. On the other hand, would not the figure insensibly gain dominion over him? "It's I am the real one, you know!"

Who said that?

"Reason, my boy — reason. We have been making a bit of a fool of ourselves to-day; but we shall square accounts yet. We are going to assert our manhood, freedom, independence; to accept slights and insults from no one—not even from Providence— eh? That was all very pretty about immortal

love, and heaven, and atonement, and the
rest of it; but to a man of the world in his
sober senses—eh? Now, Vivien had the
right stuff in her; we can talk about accidents, but we know well enough that she
had the proper pride to arrange what should
happen when the game was up. As for
Yolande—"

"You lie!" said Strathspey; but the effort
left him flaccid, and the other flowed on.

"Plain, straight-out reason, my boy: see
things as they are, say what we know; no
more sentiment and humbug—it's gone too
far for that! She was a delicious creature,
Yolande; innocent, if you like—physically
innocent; but what does that amount to?
We made a fool of ourselves there; she was
the same at bottom as all the rest of them,
and she would have preferred to have us
show up a little more . . . virile—eh?"

There was a guttural noise, such as comes
from a creature half-conscious under the dis-
secting knife, but no words. A change had

taken place: that which had seemed the phantom was now the reality, and flesh and blood had become the apparition. The initiative was with the former.

"What have I to do with this Pietistic scarecrow, made up of moral and social conventions? I am the true life! Liberty forever! Wickedness is a word to scare monkeys with, not men! There is no other God but me! Come, you sanctimonious hound, I'll make an end of you! Follow my leader—the old school game! Do you know your catechism? 'What is good?' Whatever I like. 'What is truth?' Whatever I say. 'What is purity?' Purity!" There was a low, sagacious chuckle. "Purity, my dear, is grace before meat!"

Down the veranda, through the door, along the hall, into the bedchamber. Dark as pitch; but we know that the mahogany bureau stands between the windows at the end of the room; the candle is on it; and the other thing is in the upper right-hand drawer.

He shut the door softly behind him, and for a moment stood alert just within the threshold, scenting (as it were) this way and that through the darkness. Satisfied that the coast was clear, he moved forward, and his bearing underwent an odd change. The hitherto erect and well-carried figure seemed to throw aside its human consciousness as an irksome burden; it became loose-jointed and ignoble; the body stooped forward from the loins, the arms dangled in front, the knees were bent, and the head lurched grotesquely on the neck. He began to forge swiftly hither and thither, with an irregular, ape-like gait, and with no other apparent aim than the indulgence of a vague animal impulse. A meaningless grimace was set upon his features, and from his mouth came ever and anon a clucking noise, like that made by liquid escaping from a jug. Mask and domino are poor disguise compared with that wrought upon the body by the distortion of a human spirit.

The room, as in all one-storied West Ind-
ian houses, was ceilingless, and the naked
boards and rafters of the roof rose in a peak
to the ridge-pole. The windows were un-
glazed openings, protected by green jalou-
sies with widely spaced slats. All at once a
strong gust of wind came through the shut-
ters like a sigh, and was followed by the
dash of heavy raindrops on the dry shingles.
At the same moment a large bat, whether
in pursuit of an insect or carried on the current of air, darted unseen through the gap-
ing slats, and wheeled its noiseless, nervous
flight round and round in dizzying circles.

The other occupant of the room halted
abruptly in his lope, and crouched, listening,
with upturned ear.

His mind, at this juncture, was like a
dwelling shaken down by earthquake, in
which various records of human life are
pitched together in weird inconsequence.
The noisome growths and reptiles of the
cellar are mingled with toys of the nursery

and ornaments of the drawing - room; a snake crawls out of the damask sheets of the baby's cradle, and a toad hops among the books and engravings of the library; the stench of the cesspool unites itself with the scattered perfumes of the boudoir. The owner meanwhile stumbles, helpless and bewildered, amidst the ruins, lantern in hand, the hovering light from which falls now here, now there, and whatever it reveals seems for the moment to characterize the whole. So, in this man, was the order of memory displaced, and the relation of states confused; and processes of thought had fallen to be mere impressions stimulated by the flicker of chance suggestion. The results were fantastic.

The moan of the wind-gust brought before him the death agony of a man he had once known; but the staccato impact of the raindrops became the multitudinous pattering of innumerable fairy feet scampering panic-stricken over the hollow gable.

The sound of the elfin stampede died away, a squad of belated fugitives hopping hurriedly in the rear. Then all was still again.

"Fairies! No wonder they run; this is no place for them. Dead men are kept here. They said the fairies were dead, too; my mother told me that. Poor Frank! what a cropper he came—from the fourth-story window! Vivien is dead, too. I killed her, though she lied about it. But Yolande killed me, but she won't know it till to-morrow. Are you there?"

The soft wing of the bat, eddying invisible about him, had swept his forehead.

"Are you there, mother dear? Don't go, please, mother; horrible things come to me in the dark. I shall light the candle then. A gentleman can't cut his throat in the dark. Did you hear that? There is a man here wants to kill himself. The fairies ran away. It's in the upper right-hand drawer; low down on the left is the place, an inch above the collar-bone. But we must have a light ; no bungling, you know ! Listen—it's no dream, I tell you ! He will kill me too !"

He crept warily to the bureau, and fumbled there for a while. He found the matchbox, and hurriedly lit the candle. The flare of the flame dazzled him at first, but he felt for the razor with his right hand, at the same time tilting the toilet-mirror so as to reflect his image. He stared blinkingly into it.

There are moments in life when the most appalling sight a man can behold is the likeness of himself. Could a murderer catch a glimpse of his own countenance at the instant his hand is lifted for the blow, his hand might well drop paralyzed. The ghastly incongruities of delirium, confounding the innocent child with the monstrous suicide, may work to a crisis even more fearful. Expecting to see the one, he is confronted with the other.

With a shrill scream the victim of himself dealt a frenzied blow at the phantom which grinned forth at him. The glass was shattered; the bat, terrified by the noise and bewildered by the light, blundered into the flame and extinguished it.

For a while only the noise of quick and heavy breathing disturbed the silence of the midnight room. Then was heard the voice, as it were, of a little boy, quavering out his prayers to his Father in heaven, at his mother's knees. The sacred, tender words faltered and halted, and subsided into inarticulate murmurs, as of a child falling asleep. His ugly dreams were put to flight, and peace brooded over his cradle.

The fairies returned. First one, then another, alighted upon the roof; then came battalions and armies of them. Their myriad trampling became a steady roar of muffled music, soothing to distracted brain and tortured nerves. All night long they held high revel, and even the gray ghost of dawn dispersed them not. But sin and death had taken flight.

XIII

"Vain for thy lost Flock thy Grief,—
Thine own self thou art the Thief.
More than Loss shall he regain
By whose Lamb his Wolf is slain."

"WHAT day is this, Thomas?"
"Mornin', massa! Dis Friday, massa—yas, sah."

"Are you sure?"

"Oh yes, sah. You been ve'y sick, massa; two, three days—yas, sah."

"Friday! Tell Martha to make me some coffee; something to eat. What's that noise I hear?"

"Dat de river, sah; river down, sah; couldn't get no doctor come; rain two, three days, sah; say de bridge gone, massa."

"Friday! What time is it, Thomas?"

"T'ink 'bout nine, ten o'clock, massa."

"Well, tell Martha — you understand.
Look sharp, now!"

"Oh yes, massa; glad you better, sah—
yas, sah!"

When the man had gone Strathspey
raised himself on one elbow and looked
about the room. Everything appeared as
usual, except that no sunshine fell through
the windows, which faced the east. Ah, it
had been raining, and was still cloudy. Friday! He was in bed; had been ill; certain-
ly, he was weak as a rag. How was it? His
brain was like a barren country, in which no
thought would sprout. Tuesday—yes; but
Wednesday, Thursday? And this was Friday.
Round about this central point of mystery
his mind circulated like a fascinated animal.
He got out of bed at length, and, with as-
tonishment at his physical weakness, made
his way to the bureau. No distinct idea
took him there, but he vaguely fancied some
helpful hint might offer itself in that neigh-
borhood. The looking-glass was broken,

and forced from its supports; the fragments
of glass had been gathered up and piled together at one side. Beside them lay the razor without its case. Its place was in the
right-hand drawer. Pondering fruitlessly,
Strathspey opened this drawer, and saw,
amidst a confusion of articles, the envelope
containing Vivien's letter. He seized it as
a clew, and dragged himself back to bed.
Some rose petals fell out of it on the sheet.

Though the scenery of the memory is
continuous, only such passages as consciousness authenticated remain accessible to the
mind. Strathspey could trace his acts up to
the time of his return to the veranda after
changing his dress; after that the reins of
will had been wrested from him by some il-
legitimate agent, and he had been driven he
knew not whither. But during this blind-
fold career the bandage, so to speak, had
once or twice slipped aside, giving him a
glimpse of the situation. Such incoherent
impressions, however, explained nothing—

they but served to imply some sinister predicament. He had been whirled headlong
through the Bottomless Pit, from which
some influence as unknown as that which
had plunged him thither seemed to have
snatched him back alive.

But though the circumstances escaped
him, the effects remained. He was not the
man he had been. In place of intellectual,
he now had vital knowledge of human impotence and divine power. The period of
reasonings was past, and, like a child, he
cared only to see good and to do it. "I am
nothing—God is everything," was the creed
he felt, and before it questions of justice and
compensation evaporated like mist in sunshine.

Desert implies reward; but how should he
who of himself can do nothing be rewarded?
God alone works in man, and pays Himself
no wages. But though He does not reward,
all is His gift, for it is the gift of life, which
is Love. Over against the heavenly fulness

stands that void of death which is man. The fulness yearns to give itself to, to be swallowed up and disappear in, the void and become as the void's own; so that while the fulness alone is, the void alone may appear to be: for thus to do is the genius of love. Death cannot earn, but it can receive, life; and only when it insanely prefers the death which it is to the life which would kill that death is eager heaven kept waiting at its sullen gates and the creative moment delayed.

Nothing final happens here, because mortal man is equipoised between good and evil, and may to the last freely incline either way. Strathspey, if he would, might still descend from the hard-won aërial turrets to the sensual cellars of his house, and forget in earthly gluttony the apocalyptic vision. His best guarantee of safety was his recognition of this truth, and, as he lay musing, he told himself that he had no strength in himself to resist temptation, and humbly hoped God would abate the power of the enemy.

Meanwhile he shunned forecasts and casuistry, and was content to do what lay next his hand. As the sick man dreads poison, so did he dread to disguise or in any way manipulate the truth: let it flow uncontaminated by human prudence or compassion. Whatever it destroyed was well lost: nothing else could bestow its blessings. He that trusted to its eternal current, though losing all else, would preserve what of his cargo was of avail in the world of things incorruptible.

When Thomas came back with the coffee his master said, " Have the mare saddled and at the door in half an hour."

"Yes, massa. Beg pard'n, massa—you goin' tak' a ride?"

" Why, I think of it, Thomas. It would need a worse illness than I have had to prevent me sitting a horse. I was brought up on horses, Thomas. Don't be uneasy."

"Yes, massa. Ain't no trouble 'bout sittin' de ho'se, sah. It's de roads. Dey's mighty bad dis mornin'; don' t'ink yo' git ve'y far along dis mornin', massa ; no, sir."

" Oh, that's the trouble, is it ? Yes, I remember now ; you said the bridge had been carried away, didn't you ?"

" Oh yes, massa."

" Well, I'll have to find some other way of getting across, then. I can ride up to the place the river starts from if nothing else will do. You know, Thomas, where there's a will there's a way. Tell Martha the coffee is very good. I feel much better. Be off with you now !"

Thomas went away with obvious misgivings. He knew more than his master about the effect upon tropical rivers of tropical rains; but he had said all he could. While aggressive to maintain against all comers that his buckra could outride any other white man on the island and accomplish impossible feats without trying, yet when it came to crossing a furious torrent thirty yards wide and as many feet in depth without the aid of a bridge, he permitted himself some private doubts. He confided them to the mare only, whom he prepared with especial care for her journey, finally leading her round to the front with a despondent air, as if he feared never to enjoy another opportunity to lavish on her those attentions which she was not more blessed in receiving than he in bestowing. Nor was he comforted by the evident impatience of the beautiful creature to be off. She danced along with so light a hoof that one could almost believe she could cross a river dry-shod; and she tossed up her delicate head, as much as to say that air was her proper sphere and she condescended to earth only out of regard for etiquette. She and her rider—Thomas sadly reflected—were a pair afraid of nothing, and never in such good spirits as when about to perpetrate some such monstrous indiscretion as this.

Strathspey, however, was far from regard-
ing as a perilous escapade the present expe-
dition. His habit of serio-comic dialogue
with the old darky had led him to humor
the latter; but he had never seen a tropic
river in flood, and knew not what it por-
tended. He had forded streams in other
lands, and feared not getting his girths wet.
But in fact he wasted few thoughts on the
matter, his mind being bent on Yolande,
not as forecasting their interview, but as a
plant struggles through the soil to the light
by the instinct of its life. To stand idle was
not his cue, and in order to know what were
best be done, and how to do it, he must see
her, if only to agree with her to part. Whatever else was obscure, at least they must understand each other. Until this colloquy
had taken place all was at pause.

After dressing slowly he felt exhausted, as
with a day's hard work. Those fifty or sixty
hours of illness had robbed him of the pith
of years. But his mind was abnormally

lucid and sensitive to impressions. He had
had a similar experience in childhood. Until he had entered upon the athletic life
which he had kept up through college and
never laid aside, he had been nervous and
delicate, suffering much from noises and
earthly frictions of all kinds. He had per-
ceptions which none round him understood
or shared, and which were far from welcome
to himself. For example, he would see his
companions environed with a sphere, dark,
bright, or colored, and attractive or repul-
sive, as the case might be. These airy radia-
tions or envelopes determined his personal
likes and dislikes, often in an inconvenient
manner. Sometimes, again, in the midst of
indifferent talk or occupation, he would suddenly see places at a distance and persons
whom he knew doing things there, later in-
formation uniformly confirming the correct-
ness of these visions. More rarely he would
be transported in spirit to scenes strange to
him, which he had no means of identifying;

and occasionally in seasons of solitude and reverie he had beheld beings and places which he felt to be not of this earth, though they had a perfect reality of their own.

All this had disturbed his immature mind, and he had concealed it from his fellows like a sin, lest they should ridicule him. By nature he had not been fond of exercise; but he had given himself with ardor to out-door exercise as soon as he was told that it would "cure him of his nonsense," and the prescription had not failed. The disease (or faculty) had not returned till now, when for the first time his physical stamina had col-lapsed. As he buttoned the belt of his Nor-folk jacket he saw, through twelve inches of brick and plaster and a hedge of pimentos, Thomas stealthily attach an Obeah charm to the mare's surcingle as a security against disaster; and while putting on his cap and taking his riding-crop from its hook on the wall he caught himself muttering, "The cocoa-palm by the gate will fall as I pass," repeating the words over and over mechanically, as a child memorizes its lesson by rote. He shook his head, laughed, and went out.

The mare became all palpitating springs and electric vibrations as her master gathered the reins in his left hand and put his foot in the stirrup. When he was seated he turned quietly to the old groom, who, with his lean black arms crossed over his breast, was ducking and bobbing and covertly rejoicing at having slipped a curb between the teeth of Fate, and said:

"Thomas, take that thing out."

"Yes, massa. . . . Beg pa'd'n, massa?" faltered Thomas, knowing that it was impossible Strathspey could have seen the "charm," which, indeed, was nothing but the third toe of a chicken wrapped up in a bit of rag cut from the shift of a suckling babe and secured with a piece of curly wool reft from the head of a bride just before she crossed her husband's threshold, and was thrust under the surcingle on the right-hand side, where it must be quite invisible. Remembering this, Thomas rapidly reflected that his act could not have been detected, and determined to brazen it out. The babe of the shift was less innocent than Thomas looked.

"Take it out at once!" Strathspey repeated, repressing his smile and forcing his brows to frown. "For shame, sir! Your minister shall know of this. And don't you know that folks whose lives are saved by heathen charms are bound to lose their souls to the devil?"

"Massa 'Thaspey," replied the negro, sadly, removing the offending trinket, "a gen'-mun like yo', sah, dat sees t'ings dat can't be seed, he ain't in no danger anyway. But de poo' mare, she ain't got no soul for de deb'l to take; so I t'ought no ha'm to save her be'n' drownded, sah—dat all."

"She shall come back, whatever happens to me," answered the master, with a kindly laugh; and he rode away.

XIV

"As the Waves are not the Sea,
  Bole and Branches not the Tree,
  So of Thee I naught descry
  Save what Self and Sense deny."

IT was a morning such as is seen only among tropical mountains in the rainy season. The atmosphere was steaming with magic and mystery. Pale mists were drawn across the profiles of the peaks and again snatched aside, as the diaphanous gauzes of Oriental dancers now reveal, now hide, their dusky undulations. Here a wilderness of cloud brightened intolerably in a white tide of sunlight, and yonder a foggy shield was lifted between the beholder and the source of light, rimmed with splendor and radiating glory. At times the rider seemed to float above silent oceans of fleecy vapor, and anon through the centre of the opaline whirlpool would appear dewy valleys reaching far down into the sunlight of a warmer world, or glimpses of romantic heights clothed with fern and crowned with palm. Vistas of remote defiles gleamed out and vanished. Once a white-walled dwelling, the culmination of a pyramid of distant verdure, shone forth isolated, as if seen through an opening in the sky. In lonely passes the long, sweet double whistle of the solitary filtered through the hush, intoning the melodious pathos of unheeded nature. It seemed at last as if the solid earth were hastily remaking herself after having been dissipated overnight, and, being rashly surprised before her toilet was completed, had not yet donned all her garments or even condensed herself from the atmospheric back into the substantial state. Nothing would get in its right place. She tried a valley here, a mountain there; no; then let them change places; but that was hardly satisfactory either! And here was high noon at hand and all those seas, archipelagoes, and continents still in disarray! "Ah!" panted the lovely planet, "if ever I get my equator round my waist and my snow-cap on my head again, never more will I resolve myself into my elements!" Unlike some more sophisticated beauties, she did not know that there was in her disorder something yet more enchanting than in her precise attire.

Strathspey rode at a foot pace. The private road on which he was journeying was, like most private roads in the island, steep and rugged, and the rains of the past days and nights had brought into prominence all its thinly disguised evil of sharp stones and treacherous crevices. Moreover, he had given himself time and to spare. Four o'clock was the earliest hour at which he could present himself at his destination. He meant to linger by the way and prepare himself, so far as he might, for the interview. Perhaps, too, he might have to make a detour in order to arrive below. And though the air and scene revived him, he was in no trim for hard riding. He must husband what strength was left him.

Momentous though the coming interview must be, Strathspey noticed, not without surprise, that his mind and heart were singularly free from preoccupation and anxiety. He ascribed this serenity to his physical weakness, which is apt to let cares smooth themselves out for lack of energy to exasperate them. But he was happy as well as calm. Not that he hoped for any specific temporal felicity; rather did he feel a presentiment that what he had of late so passionately craved was not to be his. But he was happy because he had ceased to aspire to personal gratification. His eyes were turned away from that petty complex of desires and fears that he called himself towards a larger self, in which he now discerned the veritable contours of his human nature. No harm could befall this larger self, for it dwelt beyond the reach of mortal vicissitude; nor need it strive after blessings, since it was the form which real blessing spontaneously assumes.

He loved Yolande not less, but to a height and depth far greater than before; but the question of winning or losing her no longer occupied him. Already was she his in the sense that the best he was capable of was his; and she was not his in the sense that no one can claim ownership in immortal treasure, but must be content to cleave to it as to a saving and uplifting hand. On such high terms the personal equation is either cancelled or survives but as the memory of a superseded expedient.

Although, therefore, she was his constant thought, he concerned himself not as to what he should say to her or she reply. Free and glad were his meditations; he and she were parts of a whole whose orbed complete-

ness could not be marred by accidents of
time and space; though zenith, nadir, and
all the ages intervened, the curve of their
arc was not distraught; it was secure as the
rainbow, because, like that, not human will,
but heavenly law, was its warrant.

He found a new delight, as he rode along,
in watching the beautiful fantasia going on
around him. Grown people are so used to
burden themselves with the gloom of their
mental scenery that external nature hardly
penetrates them. But now, to Strathspey,
these shadows and sunbursts, these heights
and dells, trees, birds, and all other particulars, became not visible only, but transparent: answering to truths and affections inherent in himself, and thus forming a living
language—an eternal and palpable Word of
God. Nature was the contents of Man pro-
jected by his Creator upon the screen of
sense, as the hues of the spectrum are the
analysis of the ray of white light. Nature
was thus because Man was so; a change in

the latter would modify the former. The material fixity was not the reality, but merely attested the constancy of the divine-human relation.

What health and refreshment are in the outward look! What a transformation is wrought in these squalid little interiors when the windows are thrown open, the doors lifted from their rusty hinges, and the sun and breeze invited within! In they come, laden with bird song and flower fragrance; the dingy old pictures that once seemed so fine, the tawdry decoration, the smirking furniture, the straitening walls and stifling ceilings—how poor are all these painful devices and accumulations now! What barriers do we build against heavenly influx; in what cellars do we cower from it; with what snaky twistings do we wriggle away from it! What labors of Hercules do we not urge to preserve in our hearts that dull pain created by the hopeless struggle to stand on the summit of our own molehill and believe it the crown and centre of the world!

The pen or estate appertaining to Strathspey's dwelling was of no small extent, and the winding road which traversed it was some two miles in length. It crept this way and that, avoiding a rugged spur of the hill there, here skirting the brink of a deep gully or trench in the crumbly soil, twenty or thirty feet down, in the usually dry channel of which now rushed a turbid torrent. Sometimes it passed through groves of ebony and logwood; sometimes it scaled a naked mass of rock, or stole beneath the leafy arches of a dusky dingle. A gray mongoose undulated across the path; dull cattle stared stupidly at the rider as he passed; a black pickaninny with a huge basket of vegetables on its head pattered by him with round shining eyes and a chirp of "Marnin', massa!" At length he threaded a plantation of bananas, drooping their broad green banners, and came in sight of the gate of the enclosure, at the foot of a declivity.

Beyond the gate the high road was visible to the right and left for a distance of a quarter of a mile or more. On the hither side of the entrance grew a tall cocoa-palm, a landmark far and near; for these trees are seldom seen on the heights of the island, and bear no edible fruit so far from the sea. The palm stood on the verge of a little terrace a few feet in height, now almost submerged in the waters of a pond which had been formed there by the rains.

It made a pretty picture; the towering tree reflected in the shining mirror. Strathspey glanced at it as he guided his mare down the awkward footing of the slope, but did not recall at the moment his recent ominous prevision of it. He was asking himself whether he would be able to open the gate with his riding-crop, or whether he would have to dismount for that purpose. He halted a moment to look up and down

the stretch of high-road, should perchance
some errant darky be within hail. No human creature met his eyes.

"If I'd had my wits about me, I'd have
chartered that little pickaninny with the basket," said he to himself. "As it is, I'm
afraid I'll have trouble. The mare is as
restive as a water-beetle. Cusha, old girl!
steady!"

He went forward again, patting her neck,
while she capered fantastically sidewise, her
quick, sharp ears now pricked forward, now
folded back like an angry kitten's. She
was not wont to behave thus. Strathspey
laughed a little. "Cusha, Cusha! Don't
you love me any more, because I've been
ill?"

They were at the foot of the slope. Five-
and-twenty yards more would bring them to
the gate. The palm stood less than half
that distance this side of it, on the right.
The footing here, though slippery with small
plashets of water, was stony and firm.

Cusha danced forward, three hoofs off the ground at a time.

A little gust of wind came up in haste from the west. It had nothing to do; it tossed itself among the mighty fronds of the great palm. They waved slightly, sibilating to one another. No further impulse was needed. The palm bent noiselessly towards the road, its tough old roots, long since undermined and unfettered by the subtle waters, softly slipping from their moorings in the liquefied soil. As the straight stem stooped, still retaining its stark rigidity, its impetus increased. It was timed to strike the earth at the same instant that the horse and rider intersected the plane of its arc. Horse and rider — the latter, at least, totally unconscious of death so near and sudden, came on to meet the appointment.

"Angus! the tree! Leap for your life!"

That voice, calling him for the first time by name, and never heard till now above the

gentle modulations of conversation, was
recognized in every nerve of his body and
instinct of his soul, and searched his heart
like the silver summons of a trumpet. It
kindled him from head to heel. He glanced
not aside to see the danger, whose sweeping
onset he felt, not saw. His spurs pricked
Cusha's satin sides. She knew the lift of
the rein, the impulse of the sharply muttered word. Two short onward springs she
made, measuring her distance, her elastic
muscles coiling like tempered steel; then,
light and deft as a cat, she rose erect,
spurned the earth, and flew forward. The
margin was narrow. Ere her black hoofs
touched ground again, on the farther side
of the gate, the giant flail of the palm-tree
smote the road behind her, grazing her fleet
heels in its descent. Spirit of Antæus,
what a blow! But it was dealt a fraction of
a second too late.

Strathspey patted her neck, his eyes
sparkling. And there, on a wonderful white

horse, erect and joyous, her face radiant
with triumph and love, and flushing with
immortal youth, her eyes greeting him as
might an angel's greet her lover new come
to Paradise, was—Yolande!

XV

"Not the Diamond, but its Light—
Not the Arrow, but its flight—
Love, and not the Lover—are
Beauty's soul and Avatar."

THE sun dilated and sent forth a mightier effulgence; the landscape expanded and assumed more exquisite proportions; its hues were soft as air and bright as jewels. The blue of the sky won you like the depth of loving eyes, wooing you to gaze deeper and deeper, indrawing you forever through warm abysses of sun-shot space towards the sources of the unseen stars. Up climbed snowy bastions and pinnacles of cloud, height above height, moulded in stately terraces and shining caves, taking the breath with tender miracles of grandeur;

poised on coigns of vantage angelic spirits
seemed to stand, robed in the fleece of rain-
bows. The atmosphere was tremulous with
waftings of faint music, distant choruses of
birds of Eden; perfumes, aromas of young
love, the breathing soul of flower-beds of
Paradise, distilled in drops of happiness into
the heart. Pæans of pure life re-echoed everywhere; you could almost hear the sap
humming in the trees, whose stirring leaves
uttered delicate syllables of vegetable felicity. There were beautiful animals in the
coverts, gliding beneath overarching sprays,
standing at gaze with spirited heads and
shining eyes; peeping through windows of
verdure; rustling unseen through serried
stems of nodding lilies. Humming-birds
broke out on all sides, like flashes of the
prism caught in mid-air and incarnated; and
hollow cups and curving trumpets of flowers,
heavy with honey, were created on the instant to feed them. Two of these tiny ex-
quisites of the air came and hovered round

Yolande's face, as if seeking to become pendants of her ear-rings.

The smooth white road, glistening like crystal, wound away along the hill-sides, now seen, now lost, receding into distances of misty chrysoprase and sapphire, passing over slender bridges that suspended their gleaming arches across purple ravines, yonder clambering venturously aloft to the ivory ramparts and sparkling casements of fairy castles gathered in the zenith. Downwards again it ran through shimmering valleys towards the tinted levels of the dreaming plain, past shadowed hamlets and clustered villages, onwards towards the enchanted city that lay twinkling and palpitating in golden haze beside the azure reaches of the everlasting sea.

Did Strathspey see all these things? There are states of the soul in which perception is omnipresent and paramount without effort; sight becomes emotion, and emotion sight. He looked only at Yolande, and all

these things were added unto him. She ir-
radiated the world around her; or that
world was she—the secularization, so to say,
of her beauty, her nobility, her purity, truth,
and goodness. When love has created heav-
en in the heart it is not strange that we
should seem girt with Paradise. We do not
need to examine it with an inventory; we
know that it must be there.

But surely Yolande herself appeared more
than mortal this morning. Strathspey could
not have told in what point she seemed
fairer, sweeter, more immortally alive and
brimming with lovely energy than when he
saw her last; but so it was. Was it merely
that he saw her in clearer light? In truth,
he had never known an atmosphere so translucent as this they now breathed; it was
more than clear—it was luminous; it was
aërial diamond. In its embrace material
substance sparkled with inherent life; there
was nothing dead in the world. Yolande,
sitting there on her wonderful horse, was not

changed. If she looked more beautiful, it
was only because he saw her better; the afternoon and evening shadows of her veranda,
down in the lower land, had impeded his
vision. And as he saw her more distinctly,
so was his insight into her nature clarified,
as if the eyes of his body and of his intelligence were identical. The meeting of
her glance with his had almost the effect of
speech—or had they already actually spoken?
The joyful surprise which his leap into her
unexpected presence had given him made
him doubtful whether or not he had observed
the forms of greeting. Had he even thanked
her for having saved his life?

Hereupon Yolande laughed. "You were
asleep, and I woke you," said she. "Is not
this glorious? See what a world your coming has made for us!"

"If it were less glorious I should think I
was still asleep, and dreaming it," said he.
"But I could never dream anything like
this. And you are here!"

" When you bade me good-night, down there, I promised myself I would ride to meet you, and give you a surprise." She paused a moment and then added, while her face lightened with a smile, " I have been with you longer than you think; you did not recognize me till now. My beloved, I shall always be where you are !"

"Was I so ill as that ? And you came to me !"

Was it possible that she had tended him in his sickness? Why had they not told him?

"You did not know me, because you didn't know yourself," she went on. " It was all dark. But it's over now, and you are well, and all is well—and right ! It was never so bad as you thought it was. And oh, my love, I love you so much more since it is all cleared up ! That secret shut your heart so I could not get into it, and yet I didn't know I was shut out. But now— there is no tiniest corner or nook in your whole heart in which I am not !"

Strathspey held his breath.

So she knew all; in his delirium he had uncovered the truth before her; and the idea of forgiving him had not so much as entered her head—she simply loved him more than ever! Her eyes, in which happiness shone like a star, told him that. He had been sick almost to death in body and soul; but if she could, without shrinking, enter his heart and welcome him to hers, he must be sane and sound again. How had he been healed? "It was no thanks to me—none of my doing!" he thought, with a strange joy. As the leper rose up clean, as Lazarus came forth alive in his grave-clothes, so from the ashes of pride and self-sufficiency had the Lord, Who still walked the earth in mercy, kindled in him a new life, and from the abysm of evil fate restored him to the freshness and morning of strength.

"All I can do is to say, 'Thank God!' I deserve nothing and I get everything," he said, bending over under pretence of adjusting his stirrup. "Seems to me," he went on, trying to clear his voice, "the only thanks God will take is willingness to receive something more from Him. Of course, I know there can be no ratio between Him and me; still, a man can't help wishing he could do something."

"Why, beloved," said Yolande, with glowing face, and a voice soft as dew, "there *is* a ratio. He meets us in our nature, which He created, and veils Himself in it, so that we may come near to Him. It is because He is there that we love each other, for Creation is love, and love needs love in return. And when we love each other we thank Him, for loving is doing His will."

Strathspey looked at her sitting on her white horse, stately and sweet as a flower. The sunlight rested on her pearl-gray habit, with facings of white silk; the breeze stirred the plume of white owl's feathers on her hat; she was so humanly beautiful—and yet there was something unearthly about her. He

felt a sudden fear lest she dwelt in a sphere
other than his, and that never would he be
able to reach or comprehend her. Stronger
than death must be the love that would hold
him to her height. If he were to lose her
now!

As if divining what passed in his mind,
she smiled with such comfort and assurance
that his courage revived, like a soldier sore
beset who sees help at hand.

" Why are you troubled? I really believe
you're afraid to be happy, sir! You needn't
be; it's what we were made for."

He laughed. " I should feel safer, though,
if I could go off and fight a giant somewhere,
like those old knight-errants. I'm like the
man in the parable, without a wedding gar-
ment."

Yolande gave him one of her slow, fath-
omless looks.

" I prayed the Lord we might meet like
this, and He permitted it," she said, in an
inward tone. " I thought you'd be glad to

know, to have seen for yourself, how it is with me here. You've had so much unhappiness, my own beloved!"

Something in her look and voice warned him; he lifted his head with the masculine alertness characteristic of him.

"There's to be a giant, then? What is it? I can fight him!"

She kept her eyes unswervingly upon him, as if to supplement his courage with hers. "A small giant, who will turn out a friend in disguise. All you have to do is to believe that I am yours and love you."

He laughed again.

"Isn't that too easy?"

She stroked the silken mane of her horse thoughtfully.

"Do you believe enough in me not to be anxious while we are together to-day? Will you be content with my saying that I am your Yolande, and I love you forever?"

The memory came back to him with a surge of passionate tenderness of that moment on the veranda when, with her lips on his, she had spoken those words into his heart.

"I'm content," he said, briefly. "Beside that nothing matters!"

But she still mused, and spoke again in the same grave, lingering tone.

"Think what we are to each other! not lifeless things, to be found and lost, but each is created the other's inmost life, closer and surer the more all else falls from us. And our happiness can never fail, for it is built on no care for our own gain, but on the will of each for the well-being of the other, and so it must grow greater through eternity."

These words opened the very heart of love, which wills all it has to be another's, and feels that other's delight as its own. Through the years of his after-life Strathspey could always recall Yolande as she then appeared, stationed on a little eminence above him, illuminated by the mellow sunshine and relieved against the glories of the sky. And he seemed to see, as it were, the sky open around her, and a gathering of many faces of pure light, of aspect resembling hers, and speaking in harmony through her voice. It did not seem strange at the time, so permeated with life were all things. But blessed is the lover who can thus behold his mistress framed in heaven and at one with angels!

As she ceased speaking the vision passed into natural elements; the seraphic faces were a concourse of fleecy clouds, and the choiring voices that inner pulsation of distant bird and insect song which in summer fills the ear without our consciously hearing it. Yolande put her horse in motion, and was once more the simple girl that he loved with all his heart.

"Come, let us ride," said she; "this is our enchanted kingdom. Come, Sir Angus!"

He caught from her tone the contagion of pure youthful joy in existence. Joy welled forth in him like a brimming river, not self-centred, but seeking to send abroad currents of delight to sweeten and refresh the world.

"Where shall we ride?" asked he.

"I want to show you the place we are to live in. Until you're ready to come for good, I shall do the best I can with it; but of course that is nothing to what it will be when we've lived in it together for a while. It's lovely, though, even now."

Without fully understanding what she meant, he rode on beside her. What a morning for a ride!

Her horse was pure white, with points of an Arab. But Strathspey, who from his youth had loved horses, and whose own Cusha was not easily to be matched, had never seen an animal approaching this in beauty and power. Cusha hardly seemed to belong to the same order of beings. This was a horse such as poets say Pegasus is— all airy fleetness, symmetry, and grace, in whose dark eyes was the fire of unquench-able courage, and yet the gentleness of a

great white dove. Wings he needed not;
though when Strathspey was not looking
directly at him, he could half fancy a feath-
ery sweep of snowy pinions which, with a
single wave, could send horse and rider
heavenward through the diamond air. He
seemed made for Yolande, so perfectly fit-
ted to her were his spirit and splendor. If
her stainless mind had conceived and given
body to an ideal steed, thus and not otherwise must he have appeared.

Cusha, who had never been lacking in
courage, was at first not like herself in the
presence of her new associate ; she was much
disturbed, and trembled perceptibly as she
moved. Noticing this, Yolande spoke to
her in a soothing voice by name (how did
she know her name?), and soon the mare
quieted down, and kept on as best she might
beside her shining companion.

"What an air this is!" exclaimed Strathspey, taking in a long breath of it. "When
I started out this morning I was feeling

limp and shaky as an old lay-figure; but now I'm elastic and keen as a boy. I could ride with you right up the side of that great cloud, and jump off the top into the blue sky! Is it a cloud, or is it a snow mountain? I never was alive till now!"

"We'll visit the stars together," returned Yolande, "and drive comets in our chariot, four-in-hand. Delightful people live over there in the Pleiades, and one of the planets there has nine moons. Then there's a place in Orion where we can sit out on the great silver terrace after sunset, and see a solar system being made, over opposite."

"And how shall we get home at night?" inquired he. "Shall we coast down the zodiac on a meteor?"

"We can make our thoughts into an eagle, and ride in the warm feathers between his wings. Nothing else can carry us so swiftly, or keep us so comfortable through the cold place on the other side of the Milky Way."

"And how homelike it will seem when we

have passed Neptune and Uranus, and see the lamps lighted in Saturn and Jupiter as we pass by! We must keep our eagle well in hand, or he will plunge us into the sun. I think I'll have a net stretched between Mars and Venus, in case of our forgetting."

They looked at each other and laughed. "It's a small universe, after all, compared with our own!" said she, sending him a heavenly glance. Paradise rioted in his soul.

Down a gentle descent they rode into a vale of fairy-land. Slender trees spread delicate boughs over their heads, laden with large blossoms. Through these the light, descending, cast rainbow glows upon them. Now he saw a rosy flush envelop her as she was swept along; now she plunged into an effulgence of aërial gold; now for an instant she was bathed in amethyst; and anon a snow-white splendor was shed around her, and suited her best of all. To right and left meanwhile opened myriad-columned aisles of a sylvan temple, resounding with stormy ecstasies of bird music; and yonder, surely, the pearly flank of a wood-nymph glanced amidst the verdure, and the tanned shoulder of a smiling pursuing faun. All nature, at times, puts on a human glamour, and leads a dance of delectable masqueraders through her mystic solitudes. Horny-eyed terrestrials see them not, but to the fine perception of lovers they are exquisitely visible.

Emerging from this glade, they skirted the base of a tall cliff, and came suddenly upon a rocky pool, into which leaped joyfully down the frosty rush of a cataract. The terraces of gray-stone over which it tumbled had become clothed with arras of iridescent moss, on which gem-like drops vibrated; torrents of fine-wrought maidenhair poured from the oozy clefts, and giant ferns spanned the basin with arching fronds. Glancing over and between enamelled bowlders, the stream kicked up its silvery heels and frolicked across the road, to disappear in deep-tinted sedge on the other side, setting the

tall stems of purple irises and scarlet car-
dinal - flowers a - quiver. To this spot sunshine came but in golden disks and patches,
variegating the transparent green of the
shadows. But glancing up through the in-
terstices of broad, enroofing leaves, you could
catch glimpses of a velvet azure sky.

Cusha stooped her pretty head to drink,
drawing the sweet water into her silken
throat with pleasant sighs; but the white
steed barely tasted it (out of courtesy, as it
were), doubtless preferring to slake his thirst
on the heights where the clouds of heaven
are first distilled into liquid crystal. Meanwhile a colony of purple violets despatched
an embassy of priceless perfume to Yolande,
and a blackbird, too shy to be seen, trilled
out a tumult of melodious welcome, which
the skilfullest human musician would have
tortured his instrument in vain to echo.

"What is that delicious whispering undertone that flows in every few moments?"
asked Strathspey. "Except I know that

the sea is miles and miles away, I should hope it was the ocean surf upon the shore."

Yolande lifted her chin with a princely smile.

"If my beloved wants the sea, he shall have it," she said. "Didn't I tell you this was our enchanted kingdom, which serves our wishes in all things? Come with me."

She cantered on across the brook, flinging up a glitter of spray as she passed, and so forward to where the road curved round the profile of the steep, he following. On doubling the point, there was revealed what seemed a miracle. A deep bay, hitherto concealed by an intermediate promontory, had made its way far inland from the general coast-line, and brought its blue-green depths of waters almost to their feet. The shore was precipitous, and the road went in and out along the face of the sea-front at a height of some fifty feet above the tide. The waves lapped narrow beaches of coral sand, and great fragments of coral rock rose

up islet-wise out of the flood, tufted and
fringed with tropic green. Looking down
from their elevation into the sheltered in-
lets of the bay, they saw below the surface
the luxuriant color and strange graces of
life under sea: fish, blue-tailed and orange-
finned, or rose-pink from stem to stern, with
keels of silver; creatures like crystal bells,
with long-depending streamers, purple and
gold; anemones swaying their jewelled ten-
tacles sheaf-like in the translucent currents;
great shells, rosy-lipped and pearl-spired; sea-
weeds of all hues and shapes, beneath whose
shelter weird crabs gathered their skeleton
claws in ambush. And then they looked
farther off over the glossy backs of turquoise
heavings and sapphire subsidings, a mile or
more, to where the outer reef turned to long
lines of snowy thunder the rolling onset of
ocean. Farther yet the dark-blue line stood
clear against the pearly pallor of the horizon,
whence blew a breeze full of such tameless
life as made the blood caper in the veins

and the heart yearn with mysterious long-
ings to sail forth and be lost in those august
solitudes.

To the left the long line of cliffs deployed,
white-footed and shaggy-browed, upon the
level reaches, fading away from greens,
through purples, to evanescent blues. From
their summits, seeming incorporate with
them, opalescent castles aspired flame-like
in the magic light. Close at hand dipped
and soared keen-winged gulls, their breasts
pure as the salt wind and foam on which
they lived.

Strathspey gazed and gazed. "Is this
the world?" murmured he.

"The world marriage makes," said Yolande, in a voice that spoke rather to his
heart than ear.

Leisurely, as though borne on happy musings, they rode along the windings of the
stately coast until they crossed a tall bridge
and saw a cleft deeply penetrating the face
of the land. Up this they rode.

Here prevailed coolness and soft shadow. A brook—a succession of little waterfalls plashing into clear pools—on whose margin blue flowers clustered and bearded mosses hung, passed downward beside them as they mounted. High up wide boughs interlaced, and every leaf was still. The riders, too, were silent, and drew more closely together. With the shadows their mood became more intimate, but more serious, also. They were passing from one vision of life to another, and were sensible of their mutual dependence. One of the secret felicities of lovers is to be still and know that love is all.

Twice or thrice, through a gap in the foliage, as through a window in a tower, they saw a wide and wider gleam of the beauty from which they were receding; but of what awaited them they could surmise nothing. Gradually the atmosphere became less slumberous, the light stronger, and little breezes ventured down between the enclosing walls to learn who visited their eyries.

The horses sniffed the air and struck their hoofs sharply on the firm white road. A few minutes later they had surmounted the ascent, and were trotting briskly along a level way, which debouched upon a lofty upland. It was a mount of vision, from which the various regions of their wanderings lay revealed, as well as others hitherto unknown.

But Strathspey, disregarding the wide-extended beauty of the past and the remote, fixed his eyes upon what immediately confronted him.

Nothing could have been more unexpected than this noble object, and yet, no sooner was it seen than it took its place among its surroundings as if the latter had been called into existence especially to adorn it. It seemed a natural growth, the key and culmination of the scene. It harmonized earth and sky, and was familiar with the sun. It supplied the human element, without which nature is but stem without flower. And as Strathspey looked upon it, tears came to his eyes; because, though now seen for the first time, it touched the chord of home in his heart. Surely the roots of his being were entwined with these foundations; memories of infancy, of father and mother, lurked in the depths of those windows; here were walls which had witnessed the games and musings of his boyhood, and porches and gables in which his young manhood had plotted conquests of the world. Whatever in his life had been innocent, generous, and good was related to the form and substance of this gracious structure, and yet all was new where nothing was strange: for here was a future interpreting what had gone before, and steeping past ideals in its own rich atmosphere. Up yonder stairways of promise his soul ascended to shining turrets of fulfilment, whence he saw, vivifying every part, the might of his love for Yolande. In the countless qualities of purity and grace, which he might dimly have desired but was impotent to create, he recognized this as her home as well as his—the home and symbol of their union.

Suddenly, without warning, his heart began to beat heavily. He felt the approach of some untoward event. He turned quickly to Yolande, trying to command himself.

"Where are we—what is this?" he asked. "Is all real that has been going on to-day? It seems silly to ask, but I've been ill—maybe I'm not straight yet. I've been taking things as they came, but now—I can't seem to account for—I don't—"

He was unable to go on. Some change was at hand. Despite an indistinctness in his vision, he could discern the face of Yolande meeting with steadfast eyes the trouble of his appeal. But her look also expressed a passion of loving sympathy that warned him his fear was not groundless.

He heard her say, "All we have seen and done is real and true, beloved. This is our country and our home."

He divined something ominous waiting behind her words, and as a wounded man would pluck from his body the arrow that prolongs the agony of life, so did he snatch at the knowledge of the worst.

"But there's something between us—I feel it!" he said, with a break of the voice.

She made no response.

"Yolande, I've felt it from the first—we cannot marry—in this world—never," he said, after a silence, in a dull tone. "I should fail— I should disenchant you—I'm not worthy. God won't permit it!"

She was still mute. A sort of helpless frenzy seized him.

"I can't give you up!" he said, fiercely.

Her eyes no longer met his—they looked beyond or above him, and her face was like marble, giving no sign. The time had come to him—as come it must to all—when in the solitude of his spirit he must meet and know God; and upon that awful meeting no other soul dare intrude.

He bent forward, closing his eyes, till his

forehead rested on Cusha's mane, which he had grasped with his right hand.

In this final struggle the temptations of the past came back with greater power. For it seemed to him that on the issue hung the fate of Yolande's soul. If he clung to her, she would go downward with him; if he relinquished her, she would go from him to God. He was now to choose whether he would lose her to heaven, or have her in hell—if where she was hell could be!

To give her up—for her own sake—but oh, to give her up!

XVI

"'Our little Life is rounded with a Sleep'—
   Our larger Life is from a Sleep, a Waking:
I love you! Hark! Deep calleth unto deep—
   'Earth is Love's Dream of Life — Death,
   Love's Day breaking!'"

"YOLANDE, are you there?"

"I am here," came the well-loved voice. He looked up. The day had become overcast, and Yolande had drawn back, so as to be out of his sight. From a ravine at his feet arose a sluggish mist; opposite, five hundred yards away, a mass of castellated rock assumed a fanciful likeness to a human habitation. He had but closed his eyes a few moments, to open them on this duskiness and change!

He too had changed. The sensation of abounding life was gone; the weakness and

weariness felt on awakening that morning
had come back with added weight. It was
as if old age had unawares descended upon
him. With the feebleness, however, had
come a composure and resignation, as of
one who, having striven long and passionately to find some great treasure in the
world, has at length laid aside the fierce
longing that dominated him, and henceforth
has no other aim than to accept quietly
whatever life is given him, and to die, when
his time comes, gratefully. All will to grasp
what had seemed his own, all questionings,
even the ache of surrender, had departed
from his soul. And as the moon rises over
the ruins of a battle-field, so a faint light of
peace rose upon ruins of what his heart had
fought for and lost, and chastened them to
a grave seemliness.

Cusha lifted her head, gazed this way and
that, and whinnied. She missed the white
steed.

"Yolande," he said again, "it has seemed

more like heaven than earth—what you've shown me to-day. I think it must have been your companionship that transfigured everything. But you've shown me too the distance between us. It isn't in me—I'm too old and spoilt—to live your life with you. You've been illuminating me with your own light, until you've made yourself (and me, almost) believe me a very fine creature; but the sober truth is I'm a commonplace sort of fellow, and I found you many years too late. You're going up, I down; every day would leave us further apart; and I won't be such a brute as to take advantage of your illusions, and tie you down by—"

It seemed to him that she spoke ; but she was still placed somewhere out of his range of vision, and after a pause he added :

"But I may be of use to you in some ways without the risk of becoming a drag on you. There were beautiful young queens in the old times ; there were beautiful young queens of whom a thousand knights asked no other

favor than privilege to fight and die for them.
You are worthier than they of devotion, my
dear, and I am but a single champion, and
not good for much ; but upon what there is of
me you can depend for as much—or as little
—as you want. The gage of favor you hung
round my neck is still, and always will be,
there. I mean, that as your friend I sha'n't
be afraid to grow old, and you won't need to
shorten your young steps not to outstrip
mine. Like the good fairy, I shall turn up
at the right moments, and at no others!
And long before I'm ready for a better world,
you will have made in this a heaven for some
honest young chap, and we all three shall
be happy and comfortable. Well, isn't that
good sense?"

Thinking it might embarrass Yolande if he
turned to look at her at this moment of giving her her freedom, he sat after speaking as
before, with his eyes on the ravine, from which
mists continued sluggishly to arise.

Her first words were so gently uttered it

was sweet to hear them, though their pur-
port seemed but a recognition of what he
had proposed.

"You are right—our marriage cannot be
here: a wisdom greater than ours has de-
cided that. But it was I, not you, that was
unfit. You have met the world and known
it, right and wrong, and you are strong and
weak as men are; but my life was all thought
and hopes and wonderings—I wasn't fit for
real things. I couldn't have made you happy," she concluded, in a tone like the sound
of love itself.

"The only fault in you is that God made
you for heaven, and you live on earth; mine
is the other way—I tried to enter a heaven I
didn't belong in," interrupted he, resentful of
criticism of her even from herself. "Thank
God, I came to my senses in time!"

"Persons whose souls belong together are
sometimes parted by their bodies," said she.
"If you and I could meet as spirits do, we
should meet indeed! Spirits don't grow old.

or have misunderstandings and disappoint-
ments. We might marry then, and have no
such hinderances as we otherwise might."

"My body is no favorite of mine," said he,
with a half-smile and a shake of the head,
"but here it is, and I must put up with it!"

"But even while our bodies are serving us
here our spirits live in the world of spirits,
and sometimes, when our earthly senses are
closed, we see and hear spiritual things."

"Ah, but after all, Yolande," he said, with
a sigh, "earth will have her day with us, and
when it's over you will have passed beyond
my reach. Let us not speak of it!"

But she persisted. "You said just now
that this day had seemed to you not like a
day of earth, beloved!"

This speech—he scarce knew why—singularly moved him. That "beloved," spoken as
she spoke it, had brought a breath of balm
from the forbidden Paradise; and the intimation of the preceding words was strange.
Why did she argue thus? It hardly accord-

ed with the philosophic friendliness he had offered, and she had seemed tacitly to accept.

"There are, no doubt, moments and hours when earth fades and something better seems to brighten out," said he; "but, as you see, the mists close round us again. God, had He chosen, could as well have matched our bodies as our souls; but since He has not done both, I must suppose He has done neither. He will care for you better than I could. Amen!"

"Ah, but we love each other — we love each other!" she cried out, with a kind of heavenly triumph. "Love is stronger than earth — he is a spirit! Tell me, beloved, is it not me and not my body that you love? Yes, I know it, for have you not loved me to-day? And if you saw me not through that veil, but as I am, and heard me say I love you, and saw me alive in a world more beautiful than that valley where first we met, and knew I was waiting for you in this glo- rious world in a house built for us by our

love, and yet that I should be always near
you, both when the eyes of your own spirit
were open and when they were closed,
nearer than on earth I could ever have
come, and safe from all perils of my own
ignorance or your noble misgivings, so that
our union even while you stayed here would
grow each hour more entire, and at last,
when time had dissolved the final barrier,
perfect, like the marriage of fire with light
—if God granted to us to know all this as
of our own knowledge, would you not be
content? Oh, my beloved, would you not
rejoice and thank Him, and understand that
in seeming to part us He had in truth made
our parting impossible? Beloved, would you
grieve to lose a shadow, gaining this reality?
Would you grieve because the waves must
wash away the print of my foot on the sands,
when you held to your heart me myself?
You have seen me this day; I am alive forever, and I am yours; but, dearest husband
that is to be, that shadow of me—that foot-

print—be glad with me that I have left it behind me, and am where no waves of time can change me. Be happy, as I am, that I am no longer in the distance somewhere outside you, far or near, but in your heart of hearts—in the heaven that our two immortal hearts have made!"

Her voice, welling forth from a region interior to mortal sense, softened into silence. He knew the truth at last.

He slowly lifted his arms, and there broke from him a great and solemn cry—a cry of anguish, of love, of awe, of fearful joy: "Yolande—Yolande—Yolande! God, my God! Oh, my love, my love!"

It rose, that mortal cry, and sank again into the depths of the ravine on whose brink he hung. There was nothing mortal to hear it, except Cusha, who started and stirred restlessly beneath him, setting forward and back her slender ears. The ghostly mists stole round him, making phantasmal the world from which the soul of his soul was gone. From below came the muffled roaring of a mountain stream. It was the same in which, three days before, he had thought to end his own earthly journey. And here, indeed, in one sense, it might be said to end. For although, during yet many years, he would be seen living as a man among men, doing well what came to him to do—remarked, moreover, as one of unusual serenity and quiet kindliness—yet on the banks of this wild river he met the only end to which the progress of an immortal soul is subject—recognition of the infinity within his finiteness. To such a one the world becomes thenceforth a contemplation rather than a struggle, and years do not seem long, filled as they are with the secret music of eternity.

Meanwhile Strathspey sat silent and inactive, save that now and then he would lean forward to pat Cusha's neck. The man in that hour found support in the simple animal's companionship. Without it, the first sense of loneliness might have been too heavy.

All day he had been led by a spirit! From the moment when his life had been saved from the falling tree until they halted on the brink of the ravine he had dwelt as a spirit among spiritual things. For that world, though unperceived, abides always not elsewhere than where we are. To us at all times, have we but eyes to see, may be visible, as to the young man who was with Elisha, the mountain and the chariots of fire.

She had taken him with her to her own home and country, which were also to be his. And verily his heart had burned within him on the way, as of old did the hearts of those who, going to Emmaus, were joined by One that discoursed with them concerning the Scriptures, revealing the spirit within the letter. And he too had rejoiced in the revelation, and had faith in the truth of the things he had seen and heard. They were spirit and life, whereof the things of this world are but shadows.

And where was Yolande? She was in her home and his, safe from harm, disenchantment, and vicissitude, awaiting his coming and preparing for it. But her shadow that must pass away—the print of her foot that must be washed out—where was that? Was it by chance that he had been guided to this spot, and left there?

He roused himself: his face flushed as the conviction dawned in his mind that upon him had been laid a sad and holy office. Upon whom else should it be laid? His gaze expanded, and he seemed to see in fleeting vision the maidenly figure on her horse galloping on the road to the mountain, ignorant of the peril of the rotten bridge, intent only upon the joyful surprise she would give her lover. Upon that bridge, tottering to its fall, what messenger of divine love veiled in mystery had met and stopped her in the narrow path! Yet no, she was not stopped, for her love, overpowering death, had, with the divine permission, prevailed to bear her on. But something of hers she had left behind on the way: and that sacred relic he was now to recover. He drew a long, tremulous breath; he spoke to Cusha; and she, sure-footed and heedful, began to descend the steep declivity by a rocky track, weaving to and fro amidst the thick-growing shrubbery.

Slowly during some hours past the waters had been subsiding. As they did so, many of the objects which they were carrying downward were left upon the banks. At a certain point in its course the stream makes a sudden bend, to pass round the base of a tall, conical mass of white limestone, which rises like a monument above the dark surrounding foliage. But its lower parts are softened by green mosses and the delicate tracery of ferns. At its foot there is a little area of pure white sand, overhung by broad leaves and bordered with quaint flowers. High on each side, shutting out the world, rise the steep, tree-clad walls of the cañon. To the left, two paces away, rushes headlong down the tumultuous torrent. It is a lovely spot, and the voices of solitude-loving birds are often heard there, embroidering a bright pattern, as it were, upon the mellow monotone of the rapids. And here a man, weary of the world, yet not hating it, might choose to sit for an hour, sheltered from the tropic sun, refreshed by the moist air, and pleased with the contrast between the foaming rush of the waters and the serene immobility of the tall rock and the dewy ferns and flowers.

Strathspey, having reached the bottom of the ravine, had dismounted, and, tethering Cusha to a bough, had crept on along the margin of the stream. Sometimes he sprang lightly from one bowlder to another; sometimes he swung himself across a gully by the aid of a drooping liana; sometimes he clung to the overhanging banks by means of the crooked roots which thrust themselves forth from the loam. He made his way steadily and without pause, as one who knows the spot to which he is bound.

He saw, first, the pointed spire of the white rock; but he was quite close to it before he came in sight of the little beach at its foot. He looked, and uttered a low and tender exclamation, not of surprise, not of horror, in which loving reverence almost dominated grief. He drew near gently, as if he feared to disturb the slumber of one who, in that quiet and beautiful nook, had dropped unawares asleep. Having reached the little white strand, he pulled off his cap and knelt down. It was a fitting place for prayer.

THE END

By MARY E. WILKINS

MADELON. A Novel. 16mo, Cloth, Ornamental, $1 25.

PEMBROKE. A Novel. Illustrated. 16mo, Cloth, Ornamental, $1 50.

JANE FIELD. A Novel. Illustrated. 16mo, Cloth, Ornamental, $1 25.

A NEW ENGLAND NUN, and Other Stories. 16mo, Cloth, Ornamental, $1 25.

A HUMBLE ROMANCE, and Other Stories. 16mo, Cloth, Ornamental, $1 25.

YOUNG LUCRETIA, and Other Stories. Illustrated. Post 8vo. Cloth, Ornamental, $1 52.

GILES COREY, YEOMAN. A Play. Illustrated. 32mo, Cloth, Ornamental, 50 cents.

Mary E. Wilkins writes of New England country life, analyzes New England country character, with the skill and deftness of one who knows it through and through, and yet never forgets that, while realistic, she is first and last an artist.—*Boston Advertiser.*

Miss Wilkins has attained an eminent position among her literary contemporaries as one of the most careful, natural, and effective writers of brief dramatic incident. Few surpass her in expressing the homely pathos of the poor and ignorant, while the humor of her stories is quiet, pervasive, and suggestive.—*Philadelphia Press.*

It takes just such distinguished literary art as Mary E. Wilkins possesses to give an episode of New England its soul, pathos, and poetry.—*N. Y. Times.*

The charm of Miss Wilkins's stories is in her intimate acquaintance and comprehension of humble life, and the sweet human interest she feels and makes her readers partake of, in the simple, common, homely people she draws.— *Springfield Republican.*

PUBLISHED BY HARPER & BROTHERS, NEW YORK

☞ *The above works are for sale by all booksellers, or will be sent by the publishers postage prepaid, on receipt of the price.*

By CHARLES DUDLEY WARNER

THE GOLDEN HOUSE. Illustrated by W. T. SMED-
LEY. Post 8vo, Ornamental Half Leather, Uncut Edges and Gilt Top, $2 00.

It is a strong, individual, and very serious consideration
of life; much more serious, much deeper in thought, than the
New York novel is wont to be. It is worthy of companionship with its predecessor, "A Little Journey in the World,"
and keeps Mr. Warner well in the front rank of philosophic
students of the tendencies of our civilization.—*Springfield Re-
public an.*

A LITTLE JOURNEY IN THE WORLD. A Novel.
Post 8vo, Half Leather, Uncut Edges and Gilt
Top, $1 50; Paper, 75 cents.

THEIR PILGRIMAGE. Illustrated by C. S. REIN-
HART. Post 8vo, Half Leather, Uncut Edges
and Gilt Top, $2 00.

STUDIES IN THE SOUTH AND WEST, with Comments
on Canada. Post 8vo, Half Leather, Uncut
Edges and Gilt Top, $1 75.

OUR ITALY. Illustrated. 8vo, Cloth, Ornamental,
Uncut Edges and Gilt Top, $2 50.

AS WE GO. With Portrait and Illustrations.
16mo, Cloth, Ornamental, $1 00. ("Harper's
American Essayists.")

AS WE WERE SAYING. With Portrait and Illustrations. 16mo, Cloth, Ornamental, $1 00.
("Harper's American Essayists.")

THE WORK OF WASHINGTON IRVING. With Por-
traits. 32mo, Cloth, Ornamental, 50 cents.

PUBLISHED BY HARPER & BROTHERS, NEW YORK.

☞ *The above works are for sale by all booksellers, or will be
sent by the publishers by mail, postage prepaid, to any part of the
United States, Canada, or Mexico, on receipt of the price.*

www.ingramcontent.com/pod-product-compliance
Lightning Source LLC
Chambersburg PA
CBHW020622030726
47497CB00007B/2363